THE BOY LOST
IN THE MAZE

For all who search
J.C.

Text copyright © Joseph Coelho 2022
Illustrations copyright © Kate Milner 2022
First published in the UK in 2022 by
Otter-Barry Books, Little Orchard, Burley Gate, Herefordshire, HR1 3QS
www.otterbarrybooks.com

A catalogue record for this book is available from the British Library

Designed by Arianna Osti

ISBN 978-1-91307-433-3

Illustrated with pen and ink

Set in FF Folk Rough and Wunderlich

Printed in Great Britain

9 8 7 6 5 4 3 2 1

MIX
Paper from
responsible sources
FSC® C018072
FSC
www.fsc.org

THE BOY LOST IN THE MAZE

A Story Told in Poems by
Joseph Coelho

Illustrations by Kate Milner

Otter-Barry BOOKS

CONTENTS

THE ORACLE

Time moves in spirals,
we are flotsam on Time's sea.
Time moves in spirals
and repeats its tragedies.

This story is about two boys,
separated by centuries,
parted by myth,
divided by reality.

Two boys hoping to be men.
Two boys severed from their fathers.
Two boys searching a maze of manhood.

One in Ancient Greece
from a time of Magic and Mythos.
One in modern London,
a city of delusion and gloss.

I am the Oracle,
your thread through this maze
as two boys start their journeys.
No step will escape my gaze.

Let me hold your hand
through these dark and winding lands.
Let us discover together
what it means to be a man.

CHAPTER 1

THEO

THEO FIRST HEARS OF THESEUS

I'm doodling again,
geometric patterns and swirls.
Sir doesn't mind.
He lets me doodle –
knows it helps me think.

Sir is silent again. He does this thing
when he forgets words –
presses thumb and forefinger
to the bridge of his nose and massages,
like memory is a small furry thing
behind the eyes that needs coaxing.
He massages and ignores
our word offerings
until memory squeals to his stroking.

"Manhood – Theseus' story
is about manhood –
about fathers and sons,
about nature and nurture,
about legacy and destiny,
about parents and their children
and what it means to be a man."

I nearly say something
before remembering
the happy family kids around me –
the two-parent kids,
big-house-in-Putney kids,
been-on-a-plane kids,
have-the-full-Sky-package kids.

I rest my head back on my arms
and listen to Sir tell Theseus' story.
I scratch a poem title
into my book...

Theseus Killed Them.

THESEUS KILLED THEM!

"Your father is a king," said his mother.
"Just lift this heavy rock –
he left some things for you
to prove you're kingly stock."

Beneath the rock he found:
sandals and a sword.
Sandals for a journey,
a sword for the criminal hordes.

Theseus walked his father's road
but the way was filled with tests.
He had to battle six enemies
and prove he was the best.

The first was Periphetes,
who was a little dim.
Theseus took his bronze club,
Theseus killed him.

The second was Sinis,
who killed with a bent-tree limb.
He ripped his victims in two,
Theseus killed him.

The third was a pig
who'd been causing quite a stir.
She was the Crommyonian Sow,
Theseus killed her.

The fourth was named Sciron,
who gave his victims a surprise swim.
He'd feed them to a monster turtle!
Theseus killed him.

The fifth was Cercymon,
A king who wrestled for a whim.
He'd wrestle strangers to death,
Theseus killed him.

The sixth was innkeeper Procrustes,
who liked everything to be trim,
forcing guests to fit his bed!
Theseus killed him.

When the killing journey was done
Theseus found his father's kingdom grim,
the young yearly killed by the Minotaur...
so Theseus killed him!

ALL ABOUT
THE MINOTAUR

We have to choose
a subject for our
English Coursework.

I choose
    to write about Theseus.
    Everything is just about him and the Minotaur.
I choose
    to delve into his journey to his father.

I choose
    to start reading
    everything I can about him.

Everything is all about the bull.
Everything is all about the Minotaur.
Everything is about muscle and horns.
Everything is about bestial strength,

                    blood and bones.

I choose
    to make my coursework
    a series of poems
    about his search for his father.

"WHY CAN'T I SEE DAD?"

I've noticed a silence
whenever I ask about my father.
Unspoken whisperings
mumble behind my mother's sealed lips.

I last saw him
in a mudslide of argument.
Told never to open the door to him,
                to stonewall his calls
                        and brick up his letters.

Seventeen now and feeling the weight
of a father's absence.
Manhood's become a rock
I cannot lift alone.

It's more than the clichéd stuff,
the girl stuff,
the body-changing stuff.
It's an energy thing.
A sit-back-and-relax-with-Dad thing.
A kick-off-your-sandals-and-trade-sword-stories thing.

But my mother's silence is immovable
as I try to pry up the edges
of her secrets.

OFFERINGS

Years of sacrifice,
years of feeding
quivering concerns
into the flaring snout of my mind.

I wanna see my dad
> *But he left us*
I don't need him
> *But I miss him*
If he cared he'd call
> *Who can I ask...?*
If he cared he'd send a card
> *Who would understand?*
What parts of me are like him?

THERE IS A STONE IN MY CHEST

Mark and I map the future
on a rainy walk home after school.

He wants to be a journalist,
his dad will teach him how to drive,
he's already picked his universities,
his parents will be at the Open Days,
his dad lets him sip raindrops of whisky
on sleepless nights.
His dad tells him how to talk to girls,
how to be respectful,
how to listen
like leaves listen to morning dew.

My mum tells me...
    "You don't have to go to university,
    no one in our family has. You'll drown."
My mum says...
    "Splash your name onto the council housing list."
My mum says...
    "Not another drab Parents' Evening –
    I'm not going again."

Dad would want me to go.
On his hailstone visits
he'd complain to Mum...
"Why can't this boy read?"

Because no one taught me how.

There is a stone in my chest
when I think of my father.
A stone I cannot lift.
A stone that settles its weight
when I visit the barber's alone,
when my body blooms.
There is a stone in my chest
that I cannot lift.

A HISTORY OF BARBER SHOPS

I couldn't find
the one Dad used to take me to.
We'd drive through the streets he knew.
He'd clap hands with the owner,
tell the barber how to handle my hair,
what line to sculpt.
Talk and laugh
in patois I could barely understand.
Making me laugh in the mirror,
winking assurance
whenever the razor bit.

The barbers near me
were Italian and Greek.
Mum tried taking me,
asking from the opened door...

"Have you got anyone who can cut his hair?"

Feeling a shame
in my mother's frustration
when the white barber
shook his head.
Part of me wonders
If he even heard
her mewled request,
defeated before it was even spoken.

Finding a barber was trial and error.
I tried one, a bull-horn bike ride away.
As I sat in the chair
the young men and women
would jump on how alone I was.
Notice they'd never seen me before.
Unprotected, they'd pounce,
asking the question
which has been a dreaded soundtrack to my life.

"Is your mum black or your dad black?"

Asking me how I saw myself,
telling me how I had to choose,
telling me how I would never be accepted.

I never went back to that barber's.

Mum found the new black barber's
hiding near the taxi rank
on one of our shopping trips.
Heaving with joy and laughter.
One side for the women,
the other for the men,
the laughter and joking
sailing the air in between.

They met me with smiles,
welcomed me to a seat
by a stack of magazines.
Instantly accepted.
Instantly family.

I breathed in the atmosphere,
the smells of cherry hair spray,
the heat from tongs and clippers,
the joy of the barber's welcome
as he signalled me with a nod
into the embrace of the chair.

Habit had me looking in the mirror,
searching for my father's wink.
Instead I found the warmth of the barber
and nestled my skull
into the caress of his gentle fingertips.

"You go Elliot, innit?"

He was a sixth-former at my school.
When I battled through the younger years
he became a playground guardian,
asking if I was all right
when bullies strayed too near,
reminding me with a smile...
"You gotta get your hair cut yeah! Come see me."

Being older, he left before me
and another barber took his chair.
Once again
I searched for my father in the mirror.

THEO'S JOURNEY
TO THE ROCK

My dad lives nearby,
a bus ride away,
a stone's throw away.
I have a weighted memory
of going to Dad's flat
during his rainbow visits.
It's been years
but his address is tagged
in my memory.

On the 14 bus after school
my weighted chest sinks lower.
I watch as the posh kids
from the posh schools
skip on and fly off at Chelsea and Kensington,
laughing about holidays,
complaining about doting parents.

I watch through flint eyes
as posh kids get replaced
by pebble-dash tourists
through London's grey.

My heart cements
as I imagine re-meeting my father.
Will he want to see me?
Will he be pleased?

I try to imagine him
telling me how proud he is,
how much I've grown,
how the impossible thing
kept him away,
    something believable,
      something understandable,
           something I could make sense of.

I find it hard to breathe
as the weight in my chest
threatens to crush.

THEO FEELS LOST

I feel lost.
Is this the block?
It looks like the block,
but all the blocks look the same.
Immovable.

I perch on a low brick wall,
waiting for the father
I remember from when I was small.
The father who'd flashed by
from a moneyed car's shadow.

I am sweating,
rivulets taking uncertain paths
from forehead to nose to lips,
dripping from acne bumps,
mapping the small of my back.

The last time I saw my father
no wise words were spoken.
He just stopped coming round.

An old woman passes,
a dark memory of my grandmother rises –
an embarrassed silence,
her disinterested stare (shame?),
my father looking more child than me.

"S'cuse me, do you know where Mr Milton lives?"
"You want number thirty-two," she says,
looking me up and down,
guessing at the thread of story
behind the question.

I feel lost
as I make my way up
the labyrinthine steps.

AT THE DOOR

The front door feels small,
looks small,
too small for a giant
of a father to pass through.
The doorbell looks tiny.

Last time I was here
I was ten.
Dad had taken me
to get lost in Trocadero,
to have jokes on the bus,
to watch a film at the cinema,
to get my hair cut.

Now I'm seventeen,
hours from having received
my mock A-level results
and I just want to share the moment
with my father.

Not that it's a great moment,
didn't get what I hoped,
didn't get what was needed,
but I'm the first to get this far
and I'm proud.
I hope he'll be proud too.

I just want my father
to tell me it's OK,
to have the father-son chat,
to pat me on the back
and say, "Don't worry, son."
"It's all right, my boy."
Just like on TV.

I press the doorbell
and wait for my father to answer.

TV REUNIONS

There are always tears and hugs,
a moment of shock
followed by a crashing
of: "oh my God"
      "It's been so long"
           "I'm so glad you came."

TV reunions are immediate,
There is no puzzled look,
no glance of suspicion,
no stepping back in alarm
as a son steps forward
to hug a father
who doesn't recognise him.

CHAPTER 2

THE MINOTAUR'S STORY

THE MINOTAUR'S STORY - BIRTH

I am born into secrecy,
born to screams and gasps,
calved into my mother's shaking arms.

For years I played alone,
ate alone,
nursed by the nurses
who dared to brave the sight of me.

My mother was a ghost,
creeping at the edges of open doors,
spying from the few windows
that faced mine.
My father was a myth,
a sound, a word –
a king.

He visited me once,
held me in his arms
and slapped me
when the point of my horns
grazed the whiskers of his chin.

From him I learnt the word Monster.

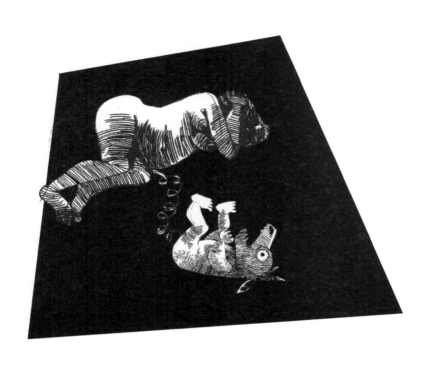

CHAPTER 3

THESEUS IN TROEZEN – THE FIRST LABOUR

THESEUS

This is **T**heseus
son to a **H**ero king
who he n**E**ver met.
On turning **S**ixteen
truth is rev**E**aled to him
his mind is t**U**rned to travel
he decides to **S**eek his father.

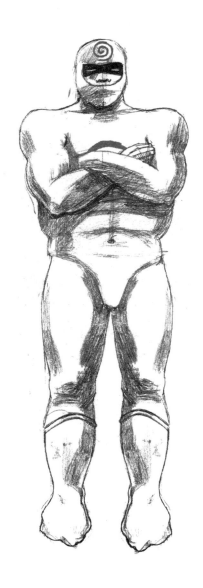

THE DRUNK GRANDFATHER KING

Grandfather has a wicked sense of humour
that he pours into every glass of wine.

"When I die, this boy will be very rich."

He hiccups, spilling his red wine
down his front.

"I am the reason this boy exists."

He always tells this story,
this lie...

"I wanted the best grandson,
so I waded into the sea
on the darkest night
and begged Poseidon
to lie with my daughter
and look! Look at my Theseus,
look at the strapping lad
Poseidon has gifted me."

He'd grab my chin
with wine-stained fingers,
spittle flicking from his
tinto-stained lips.

I love my grandfather
but I know he is a liar...

Can tell by the sadness that flits
over my mother's eyes
when he tells this story.
Grandfather always struggled
with truth and sobriety,
he smothers truth in a smile
and honesty with a joke.

But on this occasion,
my sixteenth birthday,
something has changed.
My mother is staring at me
like she has decided something.

STONE, SANDALS, SWORD

Son, I've held a secret
I have spun a smokescreen
there is something I must tell you
now that you've reached sixteen.

Your father's not a god
not a spirit of the sea
your father is a king
and he rules overseas.

See if you can stand
that stone upon its seat
there is something in the soil there
a subterranean treat.

A souvenir from your source
a little something from your sire
a subsidy of sorts
for being an orphaned little squire,

for surviving all those schooldays
sans your shepherd
your father left you something
to stop you feeling severed.

Search for that special something
sieve your snatchers through that spot
the stone is somewhat heavy
make sure it doesn't drop.

There! Sticking out from the shadow
there's the something your father stored
a pair of his smashing sandals
and his Cretan-smashing sword.

GO FiND YOUR FATHER

Your father is a king,
you should find him.
He's the king of Athens
and you should find him.

Your father is a man
who rules across the land.
He wants you by his side,
he's a very powerful man.

A JOURNEY TO
HIS FATHER

Theseus takes up his father's mighty sword,
it feels heavy and reassuring in his grip.
He dusts off the sandals,
they are a perfect fit.

With one hand he lowers
the crushing boulder to the ground
as his mother's tears
water the earth,
become the sea
that will bear her son away.

He doesn't want her tears,
refuses to be carried on his mother's regrets,
chooses earth beneath beaten feet
to lead a path to his father.

A father he's never known,
more myth than man,
more idea than parent,
        an ideal of muscle,
            a theory of strength,
                a dream of masculinity.

Theseus chooses dirt and grit,
stone and rock,
chooses to walk in his father's shoes to Athens,
chooses to map the clenched fist of the land
rather than a safe journey sailed on tears.

THE LABOURS
OF THESEUS

Theseus chose
the overland route to his father,
King Aegeus of Athens,
knowing it was notorious,
filled with murderers and cheats,
thieves and monsters.

He chose a path that would challenge him,
a path to prove himself,
a path to make him worthy
of the father who never came for him.

The first of his labours
was a Cyclops
by the name of Periphetes.
His bronze club
had pulverised a path of travellers
on the road to Athens.

Theseus arrives at Epidaurus.
A place of healing and dreams.
He stands at the threshold
of where the Cyclops is said to live...

THESEUS BATTLES PERIPHETES

A psycho Cyclops highwayman
too proud of his god-forged club
the bronze he'd use
to batter the innocent.

Each swing of his club
spells out pain on my skin
composes agony on my muscles
threatens to unknit my bones
with its verbosity.

I'm down and beat.
So, I muscle into my words
grab at them with toothed hands
forming a sentence to stop the battering...

"You don't hit as hard as I expected.
Are you sure that club is bronze?"

"IT BRONZE! FEEL IT AND SEE."

He slur-shouts as his bruised pride
hands me the club for validation.

I flip it in my articulate hands.

"You're right," I say. "It is undoubtedly
bronze."

I let my grip do the talking
as I shout its alloy through him.

THESEUS AFTER
THE BATTLE

Theseus waited for manhood to find him,
expected it to make his heart race
and his muscles bulge
as he wiped the viscera of Periphetes
from his chest and arms,
rinsed his prize club
in a cold stream.

Removed crumbs of brain and skull
from his sun-bleached locks.

Would his father be proud?
Of course he would,
his father left him a sword,
his father was known for battle.
Theseus could not,
would not appear at his father's gates
without a story,
without having cleared this tortuous road
of its criminal denizens.

He rinses the blood
from his father's old sandals,
straps the club
to his aching arms
and heads off with the sun behind him.
Feeling the tightness of his father's sandals,
feeling the drag of his guilty sword,
feeling the weight of a club won through violence.

CHAPTER 4

THEO

DAD, IT'S ME

    "Dad, it's me"
I say to a wall of fear and shock
    "Dad, it's me"
I say looking down on him
    "Dad, it's me, Theo"
I insist as
suspicious recognition skulks
into his eyes
    "Dad, it's me... your son."

BRONZE WORDS

Words are heavy in his square jaw,
barely able to hold their bronze.

He swipes lazily with the questions
clattering behind his teeth...

"What...? Who are ya?"

I'm undeterred.
Seven years change a face.
He squints through his one good eye.
The barbershop mirror wink gone.

"It's me," I say,
"Theo - your son."
With his weight on his good leg,
he eyes me up,
prepares a volley of swipes and swings...

"Didn't your mum tell you?
        I thought your mum would have told you.
Didn't your mum say?
        I thought your mum would have said.
Can't believe she didn't say.
        Thought you would have known..."

I duck, dive and weave through the blows.
His words skim my skin.

He watches each syllable
failing to land,
leans back, grunts in a bellow of air,
mentally tests the weight
of his metallic words
        and upswings with all his might...

"I'm not your dad."

THE KiLLiNG BLOW

His hallway is dark,
he feels his way down it,
peering through that one good eye.
I follow him left, then right,
up the stairs to another corridor
and round to a sun-stained front room
little changed from what I remember.

A huge frame dominates,
filled with overlapping photos of women:
statuesque women.
A photo of a boy in one corner,
at first I think it's me.
His words are hard and metallic,
nervous, unseeing words,
each one landing a blow.

                    "That little fucker is my son,"
                         he says. "Derek Junior."

"You have another son?"

                              "Er... yeah right."

He pours dark rum into a beaker
and mixes it with Fanta.

"Drink this," he demands.

"You hungry?"

"No."

"Course you are."

I push the lamb around the plate,
nibble at the yam and rice and peas.
They remind me of baby food.

"How's your mum doing?
I loved her, Theo,
she was a great fuck."

WHAT DOES IT MEAN TO BE A MAN

To say what you feel?
Let it all hang out?
To be a Don Juan?
A ladies' man?

Creator of tears.
Abandoning of children.
Alone.

To be strong?
To be violent?
To have muscles
and a chest to beat?

Creator of wounds.
Instilling fear.
Alone.

To be a protector?
A provider?
Working hard?
Moving mountains?

Creator of safety.
Building of family.
Together.

WHEN FATHERS
AREN'T FATHERS

"Did he always know, Sir?"

The question spills out of me
as Mr Addo tells us about
The Six Labours of Theseus.

I can feel everyone staring at me.
I asked too loudly,
too earnestly,
too much like my life depended on it
and now the heat is rising
as Tina and Amanda start giggling,
    as Ralph and Lenton start whispering.
        As everyone stares at me...

"Did Theseus always know
that King Aegeus was his father, Sir?"

Sir smiles at the question,
tells me it's a good one.
I take a sigh of relief
as the spotlight shifts,
as Sir reveals that no, he didn't always know.

How Theseus was lied to as well,
how Theseus was led to believe,
just like me,
that another was his father,
that his father was a God,
Poseidon, God of the sea.
All wet lies.

I think of the salt tears
cried by my mother
because of Dad,
I mean Derek.
Not my dad!
      NOT MY DAD.
Yeah that's about right, I think.

I think about Theseus
taking the hard journey
to discover his real father
and something sparks within me,
my journey has already begun.

A LIBRARY CONTAINS
A THOUSAND LIVES

A library contains
a thousand lives
in every book a life is lived.

I turn a page
I find a life
a life that looks a lot like mine.

Here's a boy
from an ancient tale
all hack and slash, I am regaled.

A fatherless son
he's just like me
a boy who takes a long journey.

Just like him
I'll map my wrath
by searching for my father's path.

A LIFE LEFT TO DESTINY

"I know the big family secret."
I lift the words up out of my chest.
Mum's at the kitchen window,
the bright sky turning her into a void,
a black hole I'm afraid to approach.

"I said, I know the big family secret..."

Her silhouette peels off rubber gloves,
stands hunched over the sink.
She draws in breath
as if trying to suck in the sky.

      "About your dad?"

she says, not turning,
and it's like a voice floating up from
some inescapable place in the darkness.

"Why didn't you tell me?"

The void shrinks a little.

      "I thought you would find out."

It's like a cold stab from the dark
knowledge of my being,
left to the vacuousness of space,
to the temper of unknowable destiny.
My ability to know myself,
left to hang like a mote of dust
in a sunbeam.

I find my words solidifying in my throat,
metallising into things I would never say,
never had the brass to construct.

I swing my words left and right,
feel the weight of them in my jaw
and watch as they fall forever
into my mother's endless vacuum.

A NAME

Hearing my father's name
on my mother's tongue
for the first time
floods my mouth with hateful saliva.

The wisdom of his name spews forth
from the locked gates of her teeth
like nothing,
like the breath it is,
impossible to be locked up,
impervious to chains.

All this time,
it sat plump
in the padded cell of her throat,
denied me.

I imagine a build-up of lies
behind her smile,
of secrets hidden in cavities.

I wait for an apology
to brace our bond,
to fix her smile in my eyes,
but it's lost in her larynx.

I can almost hear it
scrambling away down there in the dark,
can almost see the flares it sends up
shining in her eyes.

SEARCHING

I wander down Google searches
following a name.
Take paths through social media
trying to find a photo of someone
who looks a bit like me.
All lead to dead ends.

He's not a missing person,
except to me he is.
I ring a helpline and explain,
"He's not missing – but I need to find him."

The guy on the phone is soft,
understanding,
eases the taut wires
thrumming in my throat.

"We can't help, but I know a man who could.
It's a bit dodgy, but he could help."

I'm given a thread of an email,
a man with access to data,
but it will cost.

Not much – but more than I have.

"When you have the money let me know," he writes,
"and the information will be yours."

NiNETY POUNDS

How am I going to get
                    ninety pounds?
Where am I going to get
                    ninety pounds?

I mention the cost to my mother
and am met by her stumble-in-darkness stare.

At school, Tina says her phone bill was...
                    ninety pounds,
Mark flashes his latest pair of trainers, which cost...
                    ninety pounds.
Ralph saved his allowance and has...
                    ninety pounds.
Lenton has two new computer games totalling...
                    ninety pounds.
Gavin boasts about how he mugged some kids and has...
                    ninety pounds.

I just want to meet my dad
but I can't
because I don't have...
                    ninety pounds.

STRIKE

The man outside the Arndale
is round as a bowling ball and just as kind;
he's a ham-turkey dinner.
Toppling the trolleys into chains,
collecting £1 nuggets from shoppers
as he helps them into their taxicabs.

We don't have a car
so, once a week
we skittle a trolley to the taxi lanes
and wait for a black cab to roll by.
Mum always gives
the rolling man a pound or two
on top of the trolley change.
His kindness in striking
our Tesco bags into the back
puts foul lines into her mouth
when our cabbie remains glued to his seat
and we're left to dump our bags
into the gutter on arriving home.
Mum always holds the heavy bags.

The hard, shining man was my hero.
When I was a tottering toddler
his mouth was always a smiling O
beneath his two round eyes.
I wanted to be like him,
imagined the millions I'd collect
in nuggets and thank yous.

Now I'm old enough
to tackle trolleys myself.

I stand skittish in the rain by the taxi lane,
waiting for shoppers to roll by,
already counting the coins.
Ninety trolleys will equal ninety pounds.
    Ninety pounds will buy me one search.
        Ninety pounds to find my father.

The bowling ball man
bowls out of nowhere,
pins me to the outside wall
of the Arndale shopping centre.
Threatens to strike
if I stay in his lane.
His huge stomach
presses solidly into me,
two fingers raised threateningly
like he means to roll my skull.

My voice trembles apologies,
mumbles about the smiles
he used to throw me,
but he doesn't recognise me,
and the stench of BO and fags and old beer
rises off of him like the stench of
over-hired shoes.

His hulking body steams in the rain,
his flaring nostrils grunt
as his rain-ruffled hair
sticks up either side of his head.

I slip from his grasp
and run home in the downpour.
Forgotten.

DELiVERING THE LOCAL PAPER

There are ink stains on my fingertips,
I am tattooed by print,
marked by words.

A trolley borrowed from the Arndale
is my steed,
heavy with news.
I am weighted by events
that don't concern me.

A button marked 'Traders'
is my key to entry.
I am a forgery,
gaining entry on the weight of others.

My patch is large:
    Troezen Street,
    Epidaurus Close,
    Isthmian Way,
    Crommyon Towers,
    Megara Estate,
    Eleusis Cul-de-sac,
    The Athens Centre.

I know these ends,
no chance of me getting lost
as I drop papers for pounds,

collect my weekly wage
to save a path to my father...

Hours later my feet are heavy,
my trolley empty.
I heft it back to the Arndale.
My friends say, "Leave it on the street – who cares?"
Copying the bravado of their fathers,
but I can't do that.

That's when I see it,
a huge black typewriter,
an ingot of text,
left for rubbish on the kerb,
shining!
The name Corona
emblazoned in gold
beneath its striking keys.

I lift its glinting load into the trolley,
abundant with the poems I'm yet to write
and something sparks within me
as I conduct it home.

There are ink stains on my fingertips,
I am tattooed by print,
marked by words.

SAVING

I'm pulling double shifts at the gym,
delivering the local paper on Thursdays
and selling what I can at school:
read comics, used text books, completed games.
    I'm tired.

When the next pay-check comes,
I need enough to:
give Mum money for the landline,
buy a new rucksack,
pay for an address.

I've told Mum about the cost.
Her reply never reached me.

I'm alone on this hunt,
looking in the dark
for a father
who has never looked for me.

GYM JOB

The smallest of the muscle-bound men
peacocks around the weights,
pumps one bicep, then the other,
eyes fixed on the water-pull of his reflection.

I pick up the weights after them all.

> "Pick up these weights
> every day
> to gain muscle mass."

My manager has no end of tips
on how to get ripped whilst working...

> "Clean the mirrors
> using your whole body."

> "Pick up the Swiss balls
> by squatting to the floor."

> "Wipe down the machines,
> using your whole range of movement."

The muscle-bound men snigger at me as I clean,
taking their cues from the rippling plumage of
the runt,
winking whenever a woman runs on the
treadmill,
calling me names when I refuse to join in.

I muscle through the repetitions,
mind pumped for the end of the month
when I'll pick up my first pay-check,
having gained ninety pounds.

CHAPTER 5

THE MINOTAUR'S STORY – A TODDLER

THE MINOTAUR - A TODDLER

"You were born of gods and kings."
My nurse regales me with this tale
of a magnificent bull
that arose from the sea,
a heroic symbol of all that is male.

"The king loved that bull."
My nurse comforts with compassion.
"He kept it so near,
his God-given gift,
that you, his son, take after his passion."

    I spy my mother
    listening in the doorway – she never enters.
    I learnt to stop crying for her.

"Because your father loved that bull..."
my nurse tells me another story,
"he finds it hard to see you
now the bull is gone."
She tells me that he loves me sorely.

"You will be a god-king."
She comforts me with lies
when the darkness creeps
and I cannot sleep
and the shadows fall over my eyes.

CHAPTER 6

THESEUS AND SINIS ON THE ISTHMUS

DiViDED

My first combat prize
heavy in my hands
as I walk the Isthmus,
the neck of the Saronic Gulf.
I have travelled far,
so why am I not happy?

I replay the battle,
the stupid look
on Periphetes' face,
his slurred speech.
Were they battle cries
or cries for help?

Did he attack
or did he defend?

I focus on my father,
clearing the road to his kingdom,
walking in his sandals,
swinging his sword.

He will meet me
as a hero.

The screams of Periphetes
wake me at night.

SiNiS

Sinis was of two minds —
a walking contradiction,
a monstrous murderer,
a doting father.
Gentle to his daughter Perigune,
cruel to whoever passed.
Still and kind one moment,
violent and cunning the next.

He loved the moments in-between —
day decaying into night,
night screaming into day.
As a child he would pluck one wing
from the flies he picked
from half-dead dogs
and watch them spin in circles.

His mind was fractured.
Perigune tried in vain
to bind the splitting halves of his psyche.
She loved her father,
the father who named her after a moth.
Hated her father,
the father who killed.
Pitied him for the mind
that tried to make sense of its division
by splicing the world into parts.

She'd watch from the woods
as her father greeted travellers
through a half-smile,
before swiping with half a branch
from one of his half-grown pines
and then binding their semi-conscious bodies
to the trees he had half-bent to the ground.

He'd always wait
for them to awake,
for their voices to quake
as they begged to be let down.

Wait for them to feel
the tension in the bent trunks
before cutting the leashes of the trees,
unzipping his victims.

PiNE-BENDER

A scream   it sliced through the air
unlike anything   Theseus heard

The scream   a ripping
a cracking   spine
an unzipping   of body
a flaying   of flesh

The scream   it tore through him
made him weak   to his knees
made his   stomach leap
bile bubble   from the back of his throat

Theseus sees   two pine
trees   like horns
atop the   swaying
shaggy hill   from their
quivering   trunks
two half-men   strips of a man
hang

BETWEEN TWO TREES

Memories of my mother tug
whilst the mystery of my father yanks.
My journey aims to join his ranks,
my only loss, a mother's hug –
that sweet comfort, eternal drug.
Am I Father's son? Or a sperm-blood bank?
Memories of my mother tug
whilst the mystery of my father yanks.
My padlocked eyes paint her pained shrug,
her tear-dammed eyes I could never flank.
I flee their patter for my father's clank!
Memories of my mother tug
whilst the mystery of my father yanks.

PERIGUNE STARED AT THE SUN

She never looked them in the eyes,
preferring the burn of the sun's curtain.
Her father released them
with the sun at its zenith.

Perigune looked above them,
through them,
let their silhouettes
play on the burn
of her tight-lipped eyes.
She never helped, not once.
She was no good at tying knots,
said she feared splinters, heights
and the sap's volatility
whenever her father bade her climb and tie.

She looked above the victims,
through them, never at them.
Gazed at the dazzle of the sun
as they screamed,
as the trees straightened
and the flesh ripped.

She stared at the sun,
saviour and comfort,
outshining any terror.
She blocked her ears with sunrays,
blinded her hearing.
Perigune stared at the sun.

THESEUS CREEPS

Theseus creeps low,
skirting round the side of that bovine hill
with its pine-tree horns.
He takes aim at the back of Sinis' head,
with bronze shout in one hand,
his father's sword dragging in the other.
Wondering how fragile an egg-shell skull
can contain so rotten a yolk.

Sinis is admiring his handiwork,
his splitting, ripping, unzipping work,
sweat glazing his sun-aged face,
his crown-hair damp against
an otherwise bald pate.

Theseus is framed by the sun,
as two halves of a man
flounder in the wind above him.
He doesn't look up,
doesn't want to see it again.

He raises club and sword zenith high,
aiming to bash and slice
his way to heroics but is caught
off-guard, off-balance, bronze-handed by a girl.

A girl with startling wide eyes
and deep bronze skin.
She has a look about her of Sinis,
Sinis minus the mad, the brutal, the violent.
She must be his daughter.
She is as beautiful as the sun
and she is staring at him...

Should Theseus...

**strike Sinis before his daughter
raises the alarm?**
➤ **Go to page 98.**

hesitate?
➤ **Go to page 100.**

run away?
➤ **Go to page 104.**

STRIKE SINIS

This show of violence feels wrong,
against his mother's teachings.
But...
his father left him sandals and a sword.
Men are made by the steps they tread
and the swords they wield.

The girl's eyes shout "Strike!"
Wide with steel and shame,
a desire to trade places.

Theseus thinks of his father
and the man he wants to become
as he shouts the club
through the back of Sinis' skull.
Follows with a clumsy hacking slice
from his father's rusted sword
(as sharp as a spoon),
his eyes tied with hers in the swinging.

Her fleeting flicker of relief
replaced by something else,
like a wolf denied its meal,
envy and jealousy,
anger and regret, all coiled.

Theseus' eyes bounce
to the bow in her arms,
watch the resigned look
of her beautiful eyes
as her nocked arrow
pierces his heart.

➤ **Return to page 97.**

HESITATE

Theseus becomes the weapons,
all weight and length,
heavy and dull.
Words retreat from him.

His heart goads.
She is beautiful.
Loose curls framing a quizzical face
shot through with shock and hope.

He lowers his weapons,
decides not to murder her father
(wouldn't make for a great first impression).
He knows he should move,
senses Sinis sensing him,
but is caught by the flechettes of her eyes.
Her face is changing,
will she warn her father?
Strategy flanks Theseus' attraction...

RUN RUN RUN!!!

He turns to flee.
The branch comes from nowhere,
thick and sappy in Sinis' hands.

Theseus become undone by a weapon
all weight and length,
heavy and still,
blood flees from him.

➤ Go to page 102.

SPLIT

I wanted to run —
should have hit,
should have scarpered,
should have split.
Chose to hesitate,
big mistake.

A pain in my head
wakes me first,
then blistering
quenchless thirst
of a guilty sun,
think I'm done.

Hands and feet are numb,
a tightness.
I open an eye
through blindness.
My gaze meets Sinis,
nemesis!

He drools on a knife
kissing rope
that binds the trees,
bent by hope,
once they are released
I'm deceased.

Behind him, the girl –
heart-splitting.
I recognise
what's flitting
across those dark eyes,
unheard cries.

Sinis saws at rope
with dull knife.
The pine trees creak,
mourning life.
Releasing a dream –
my body screams.

**Dead end. Try another path.
Return to page 97.**

RUN AWAY

She has an enviable beauty,
I can't tell if I want her
as much as I want to be her.

Her gaze falls into me,
makes the weight of the weapons
feel wrong.

My hesitation has been too long.
Sinis is turning,
fury rolling over
the roiling folds of his face.

A hefty pine branch in his hands,
he swings it at me
with murderous arms.
I brace for it to connect
but instead hear a scream.
An arrow is imbedded in his shoulder.

The surprising girl
is lowering a bow,
a determined grit in her eye.
She mouths, "Run," and
speeds off into the surrounding forest.

Should Theseus...

follow the girl?
➤ **Go to page 106.**

stay and fight — make his father proud?
➤ **Go to page 108.**

FOLLOW THE GIRL

The air snaps overhead,
Sinis barely misses crushing my skull
with his pine limb.

I aim for the trees.
Am I mad to follow the girl?
Did she shoot her own father?

She flutters left then right,
swoops a bank
that I tumble down.
She is moon-quick,
I'm bronze-panting to keep up.

A roar splits the air behind us.

                    "He's coming… be faster."

She takes off again,
gliding turns and knife-back switches,
hovering over roots,
scaling fallen trunks.

My wheezing chest,
the mountainous weapons
staining my hands
    drag me down,
        drag me backwards.

Sinis slings forward,
his roar like the rip of fresh wood
like the crack of yielded pine.

I trip on a stump
that the girl flies over,
Sinis' roar is above me,
                    over me,
                        through me.
In it I hear the screams of Periphetes.
Crowding in on all sides,
every bush and tree
shaking in his wake,
shaking me.
My club is too petrified to lift.
My sword too scared stiff to swing.
Shame lies heavy on my tongue...
                    What would my father say?
The air thwaps,
my face is dusted in blood and silence.
She has landed,
her painted eyes coming into focus
behind her exhausted bow.
She lowers her arms,
Sinis topples
through the bushes behind me,
an arrow between the fallen trunks
of his eyebrows.

➤ **Go to page 110.**

STAY AND FiGHT

The girl runs,
pity — she was pretty.

I feel the strength
of my father's sword.
The pride of my prize club
    (The helpless look of Periphetes — NO!)

A few weeks on the road
have turned my muscles into rope.
I am tied to these weapons.
Threads of stories
woven for my father's ears,
despite the years
of fatherlessness.
I am man enough
to clear the road he laid out for me,
just to meet him
                man to man.

The thwack comes from nowhere,
through my dimming, bleeding eyes.
Sinis is branch-handed
and all goes black...

➡ **Go to page 102.**

PATRICIDE

The idea wasn't new
she had long imagined doing it
planting an arrow
through her father's skull.

But he was her dad
and no matter what he did
no matter how many he killed
she could never bring herself to do it.

His victims saw the monster
she saw the confused man
who, despite his dithering
despite his screams at night
still held the ox strength of his youth.

The strength that tumbled
her childhood into the air
and never once let her fall.

He needed help
but there was no one.
She had prayed
but Gods refused to listen.

So she did what she could
sapped her eyes shut
whenever a traveller strayed too near.

His world, for a day or two
would be whole after a splitting.
But eventually the night-screaming
would return like needle fall
and the pulling of hair
and the shouting at the sun
and he'd start bending the pines
and leashing them down.

Seeing the boy with the club
wasn't a revelation
but it did feel like a sign
like maybe the Gods had heard
that through him
they were showing her what she must do
so she did it.

Unleashing an arrow
as her father chased his demons.

PERIGUNE MAKES MAN ANEW

Younger than me and bloody scared.
I check him for wounds,
wipe my father's blood from his face.

> *"You killed him."*

I show him the red of my smile.
The act feels unreal, a gory play
with none of the red-curtain relief.

> *"Was he your father?"*

What clot of my father does he see in me?
What part of me is so gruesome?
This boy never saw the father I knew.

> *"Come with me to Athens."*

I envy his sanguine youth,
want to inject it into myself,
want to cut it out of him.

> *"You have killed your father,
> I am looking for mine."*

As he talks, I blot his face,
he gloats about his club,
lays it on thick. I take his hand.

"Where are we going?"

I lead him through the veins of trees
to the pool where the rushes beat
as he tells me how beautiful I am.

"You're safe now!"

I urge him into the water
as he tells me about the cut of pleasure
and gasps at my sudden nakedness.

"Are you a virgin?"

He tries to bandage his virginity,
I pull out from him what I want –
a seed that I will fashion into a man.

"I think I love you."

A man with no need for a father,
from a fatherless man
and a father-ending woman.

"Please speak to me, please come with me."

I will fashion man anew,
a man with my guts in his heart.
I extract what I want from Theseus

and I leave.

PERIGUNE TO HER SON

Your father shined.
Removed the branches
from my eyes and charred them.

I tell my son these lies.
A son should believe in his father.

CHAPTER 7

THEO AT SINIS SOLUTIONS

OBSESSION

I can't stop thinking
about Theseus.
My dreams transport me to him,
travelling on the road
to find his father.
                    Just like me.

And my dreams become poems
on my found typewriter.

I get obsessed.
Start making my way
through a maze of searches,
watch animations online
about his six labours, SIX!

I borrow books from the library
of adaptations of his journey.
One morning I head to the British Museum,
cycle down, hands clamped
on the bull horns of my mountain bike.

Through wind and rain
I weave London's labyrinthine streets,
just to get to the Greek and Roman Gallery.

Just to see a bowl
that has Theseus on it,
not fighting the Minotaur (for once)
but battling, striking,
overcoming every obstacle in his way,
all to get to his father.
All for the love he feels for his father.

I make notes for my coursework.
I sit with my back to the wall of room 12
in the British Museum,
scratching poems about men and monsters.

Sinis Solutions

Here at Sinis Solutions
we search cyberspace
for your solutions.

We sieve the sand-dust sea
of every enquiry,
seeking out, just for you,
the answers to
the what, when and who!

GLiMPSED BETWEEN THE PiNES

I battle the bull handles of my bike,
following my phone's blue-dot breadcrumbs:
    past Trafalgar Square,
    the slalom of Leicester Square,
    through the curves of Regent Street
    and banking the crosses of Oxford Street
    before sliding down into Soho.

The logo on the buzzer is of two trees,
feels wrong for an internet-search business.

The door buzzes,
stairs tumble me down into darkness.

"Down here," he shouts.

I pass posters for Sinis Solutions,
their advertising ditty ear-worming.

A whirring and buzzing, twisting corridor
leads to a pine-panelled room.
The swirling grain – my eyes ache
from the glare of too many monitors.

It's a studio, an office and a home.
A door to my left is ajar,
where huge brown eyes
stare out at me.
She is gorgeous!

I'm staring for too long.
Should I smile?
I should smile!
Oh shit, I'm not smiling,
I'm just staring!
Like a fucking weirdo.
Her hair is all shaved on one side,
braided on the other,
and is that glitter eye-liner?!
Shit, she looks cool, her clothes are cool,
her trainers look amazing.

She shuts her door
and I swear she smiles.

DON'T MIND
MY DAUGHTER

"Don't mind her,
that's just my daughter, Moth."

"Moth?" I say, realising too late
how incredulous I sound.

"Mother named her," he says,
rolling his pine-needle eyes.

He is sitting between two banks of computers,
made silhouette by their blaze.

"So you're the one who called?
Theo, right? Looking for your dad?"

I nod, embarrassed, and step closer.
He plays with a length of computer cord,
runs it hungrily through his fingers.
Every horror film I've ever seen
scrolls through my mind –
of murderers strangling
and cutting and ripping
and killing.

"I can do the search for you but it's gonna cost,"

he says,
and a split grin
lights up his stump teeth.

IT'S NOT JUST NINETY POUNDS

It's ink-stained fingers,
it's skittering shopping trolleys
and lifted weights.
It's the memory of a secret revealed,
of my identity reformed.

I hand over the crumpled notes.
I can remember receiving every one.
As the notes pass from my hand to his
I think of blood
passing through transfusion lines.
I think of involuntary organ donations.
I think of scales and pounds of flesh
as he stuffs the sweaty notes
uncounted into his back pocket.

HACKiNG

I give him a name
gifted by my mother
and he types,
working at one column of computers
and then the other.
Black screens of code roll
as he types at one keyboard,
the other keyboard,
both keyboards,
his fingers a blur.

Government websites
flash across the screens,
their red warnings screaming.
He dismisses them
with a cudgel of code
and a zip-tie of algorithms
as he explains to me
his philosophy.

PUBLIC AND PRIVATE

You have two digital lives,
your private and your public.
Your private is the messages to your mates,
those sweary tweet replies,
those stupid jokes,
the things you wouldn't say to your boss.

Your public
is the mask:
the suit and tie,
the good-cause posts,
the humble brag,
the holiday photos,
the exercise pose.

We spend the breath of our living lives
curating a public digital mask
behind which lie
our true opinions,
our medical histories,
our unfiltered photos.

I remove the mask –
strip the public from the private,
leave both to flap on the wind
like flayed skins.

I rip digital lives apart
and in doing so
let the truth flutter,
the truth that everyone is in fact two.

ANOTHER
NINETY POUNDS

To give you the answers that you need
I need another ninety pounds.
The internet I'll split and bleed
to give you the answers that you need.
Your father's name was the first lead
but I need more for an address to be found.
To give you the answers that you need
I need another ninety pounds.

I DO NOT HAVE ANOTHER NINETY POUNDS

You're asking for more but I am skint,
I do not have another ninety pounds.
I saved this money by delivering newsprint.
You're asking for more but I am skint,
I was humiliated by the trolley sprint,
made coin lifting gym weights off the ground.
You're asking for more but I am skint,
I do not have another ninety pounds.

THE MAN AT SINIS SOLUTIONS

Has eyes like slits.

"Can't help ya then,"

he says as a smile cracks
across his screen-glared face.

I turn too quickly,
feeling split.
Can feel the splinters of tears
rising up behind my eyes.
Can feel the anger crowing in my chest.

If I knew how to be a man,
I would demand he gives me
what I paid for.

I never saw my father
argue for what he was owed,
never learnt how to demand,
how to raise my voice,
how to stare a man in the eye.

Men see the coquettish in me,
I feel it in myself...
   the skills I learnt from my mother.
Smiling too much in male company,
looking sheepishly away.
Using flirtation as a tool
when I should be using vice.

I'M SPAT OUT ONTO THE SOHO STREETS

I'm spat out into the rain
of the conspiring Soho streets
that keep me from my father.

I shelter in the doorway
of Sinis Solutions,
the anger of being cheated
rooting through me.

I should storm back downstairs,
threaten the cracked-smile villain,
tell him to keep searching,
to give back my ninety pounds.

Thoughts never put
iron into my mouth
or brass my actions.

How could I get the money?
Londoners rush by,
pockets heaving with what I need.

At school Gavin is always
flashing money about,
boasting about the kids he mugged
over the weekend.

A woman in a suit
is walking towards me,
one of those umbrellas with wind slits
held proudly above her head.
I bet she has ninety pounds in her purse.

Should Theo...

follow the woman?
➤ Go to page 136.

**stay in the doorway and wait
for the rain to pass?**
➤ Go to page 138.

A MADNESS ROLLS INTO ME

A madness rolls into me.
I slide into the rain behind her,
images of me stopping her,
demanding the money from her,
crashing through my skull.

She is wearing a yellow mac
and holding a brown leather briefcase.
Everything about her screams money.
I imagine saying the words expected of me.
"Give me yer money."
Imagine her scared face,
her quivering mouth,
her hands fumbling for the notes
that line her purse.

I stop.
She has glanced behind her,
glanced at me,
steel in her eyes.
My heart explodes.
What am I doing!
Through this stupid daydreaming
I have inadvertently walked too close.
I feel sick.
I sort of mumble an apology
though I've done nothing.

Pass her as the rain creeps its way
into the holes of my trainers,
sticks my jeans to my legs.
I run the gauntlet to Piccadilly tube.

The search for my father is over.
I've proved myself no man.
I wrap my shame about me
and accept my fate
as a fatherless son.

Dead end. Try a new path.
➤ Return to page 135.

A MOTH iN THE RAiN

I stay in the doorway
Of Sinis Solutions.

I hear her flutter
before I see her.
She is a Spectacle.

Feel the heat of my cheeks,
Herald to her coming near.

She stands uncomfortably close,
blows a vape's nectar scent
in a Maiden Blush plume
that hummingbirds around me.

"My dad's a fucker," she says.

"So what's the thing with your dad?
How come you don't know where he is?"

I tell her my Blood-vein story,
stuttering and rubbing
the White Satin rain from my brows,
looking everywhere
but the pools of her Hawk eyes
with their Silver Y glitter smudge.
I wish I'd learnt how to talk to girls.

"I can get the information for you
if you want − .fuck my dad,
dads can be fuckers.
You sure you want to find yours?"

I nod, entranced, as her Willow Beauty
offers a Large Emerald of hope.

"Come on then," she says,
"let's get out of here, he'll be pissed
if he knows I'm giving you a freebie."

And just like that
I'm following a moth
through the rain.

SAVED BY A MOTH

We find a café.
She orders a huge hot chocolate
with all the trimmings,
then looks at me when it's time to pay.

"What? I'm doing you a favour!"
she says as I shake change from my jeans.
I'm short by a pound.
She laughs, taking a tenner
from her pocket,
and orders another for me.

We sit in the deepest corner of the café
between the clattering of cups
and the slurping of coffees.
She takes out a laptop,
black and heavy,
and types between sweet scorching gulps.
My palms sweat
as she enters my father's name,
each letter a footstep closer to him.

I can't stand the wait,
I'm tapping my legs,
wringing my hands.
I've downed the hot chocolate
and now watch while scales of glitter
from her wide eyes
drift onto the table
as she works her magic.

By the time her hot chocolate is drunk
I have an address.

CHAPTER 8

THE MINOTAUR'S STORY - A BOY

THE MiNOTAUR - A BOY

My older sister Ariadne
visits most nights,
skulking in
when the nurse and guards sleep.

She tells me different stories.
She tells me of an inventor, Daedalus,
tells me of a wooden cow he built,
tells me how it was presented
to the bull risen from the sea,
tells me of my mother's shame.

At first I don't believe her,
I rage and clomp
and fall down in tears.

"Nothing matters but truth and family,"

she says.

"You are my brother for now and always."

CHAPTER 9

THESEUS AND THE DEMON PIG

NOT ALL MONSTERS...

The villagers spoke of a beast
of flaring snout and squealing roar
a pig-like monstrous thing
that nightly skulked from door to door.

It was said to have eaten neighbours
as they slept in their beds at night
it was known to maul any man
with its vicious tusky bite.

Its body was all muscle
wrapped in scale and spine
its movements were too sinuous
for a beast considered swine.

Its body far too long
for a creature on four legs
but none could deny the piggish eyes
that rolled inside its head.

Or the nose that was most pig-like
but with a reptilian tone
its blood-snot nostrils that could smell
the fear in a grown man's moan.

Its father was a serpent
its mother – part woman, part snake
a monster born of monsters
that roamed when the world first quaked.

Theseus comforted the mourning
the bereaved and the wounded dying
he declared with an heroic air
that he would do the purifying,

of ridding Crommyon
of the beast that stalked its land
how he would skin the pig-like thing
and how its hide would be tanned.

He ran into the forest
with sword and club held heroically high
he followed the ruts of the rutted ground
hunting for the beast's monstrous sty.

The trail led him to a hut
the ground around all beastly tramped
and there within by a fire's roar
an old woman sat hunched and cramped.

"I am Phaia," said the woman
"I am the beast that you seek."
And Theseus saw from the open door
her cloven hooves transform to feet.

"I am the monster that eats the village
I am the sow the slithers in the gloom
and if you come any closer
it will be to meet your doom."

"I do not fear you," said Theseus
stepping into her lair
"I have come to kill you, monster!
to rid the village of your snare."

Phaia gave out a cackle
that had the intended effect
"What do you really know
about the people you claim to protect?

The people of that village
have done unthinkable things
and if it wasn't for my stalking
their terror would infect everything.

There were others here before them
that they slaughtered without a care.
There's a trail of death behind them
to which no war could compare.

I have tracked them as they've travelled
sowing misery and blood
and I have taken those I can
I have stemmed their murderous flood.

Now you have come to kill me
to prove yourself a man
but not all monsters have claws
and not only men protect the land."

Should Theseus...

believe Phaia and let her continue
her form of justice?
➤ Go to page 154.

disbelieve Phaia's lies, kill the beast
and save the people?
➤ Go to page 152.

KILL THE BEAST

The woman pig of snout and fear
she starts to drool, she starts to rear
as I ready myself to attack.

She rushes forth all tusk and tooth
no match for me, my club is proof
that a man does not hold back.

THE PEOPLE ARE WILD

The people are wild to see me.
They have hungered for my return.
They howl and bellow to greet me
with a feast as a bonfire burns.

I'm suffocated with dark praise –
the beast's head lies dead at their feet.
They lead me to the skyward blaze
as the drums' onslaught starts to beat.

A pack of slithering women
leave kisses on my steaming skin,
as I'm lifted by a pride of men
a new terror starts to sink in.

I'm thrown onto the fire, their only gift is pain.
Regret burns within me.
The wrong beast was slain.

Dead end. Try another path.
➥ **Return to page 148.**

TRUST YOUR GUTS

"Trust your guts," said Mother,
"before you raise your fists.
Violence tends to smother
life's natural turns and twists."

"Before you raise your fists
be sure to use your mind.
Life's natural turns and twists
are often hard to find."

Be sure to use my mind!
Mother's words flow through my head,
her voice so hard to find
as my journey piles up the dead.

Mother's words flow through my head –
I can no longer ignore my doubt.
The villagers' eyes hide piles of dead,
I'll let this monster's justice out.

I can no longer ignore my doubt.
Violence tends to smother.
So I'll let this monster's justice out.
"Trust your guts," said Mother.

CHAPTER 10

THEO AND THE CROYDON SOW

I WRITE A LETTER

How do you start a letter
to a father you've never met?
"Dear Dad" – too familiar.
"To whom it may concern" – too formal.

I've written the address Moth gave me
on the envelope, even stamped it.
I've rewritten it
a hundred times over,
typing, writing,
scrunching up and starting again.

Every aspect feels weighted.
Will he judge my handwriting?
My choice of words?
Will typing it make me seem professional?
Would that make him proud?
Or will it feel officious,
will he think I'm a fraud
or the real-deal looking for money,
like the eventual plot-line of every soap
of the bitter long-lost bastard?

I settle on a typed letter.
I long to show it to someone,
to get their opinion,
to get their support.
I think Mum knows what I'm doing
but she avoids the subject,

pops it in the box of unmentionables
next to my education and feelings,
her drunk parents, and the schooling she missed.

I don't know how to sign it.
Does signing my full name seem angry?
Like I'm making a point
of our differing surnames?
Does not putting my surname seem too hopeful?
Like I'm suggesting a gap for him to claim?

I keep it formal,
to the point,
factual. Sign my whole name,
my whole being,
offering it up
and laying it down.
This is me,
your son,
take me as you left me.

NO REPLY

Weeks away from the holidays
and my concentration isn't sticking.
My coursework deadline is soon.
I show some of my poems to
Mr Addo. He gives them
his stamp of approval,
says it's a topic
worthy of a PhD.

I can't focus.
I can't finish.
Every day I scoop up the post,
checking for a letter in an unknown hand
that never arrives.

I agonise about what I wrote,
about my choice of words,
a sinking feeling
posts through me –
that I've been rejected,
that my father read my words
and chose not to reply.

But then I excuse
my imaginary father.
A man I imagine to be tall,
with a shaved head,
handsome and strong.
Quick-witted and successful,
maybe a bit like Sir.

I imagine he is travelling for work
    and has not seen the letter yet.
I imagine that he has seen it
    but is just trying to think
    of the right words to say.

I imagine he has seen it
    but thinks it's fake.
I imagine my letter has been lost in the post.
    These and a thousand other scenarios
    track through my head.

So a decision takes root in my mind.
Once the holidays start
I will take the journey of my letter.
I will knock on my father's door.

WADDON

Another unremarkable suburban station.
It took forever to get here,
jostling on the train lines,
the bull handles on my bike
earning me tuts and scowls
from every businessperson
piling onto the train.

I wanted my bike,
needed it,
didn't want to be stuck
walking up the wrong road.

Waddon station feels familiar,
another suburban red-brick station
where the ticket booths are closed
and the machines aren't working.

Where a dead-end Station Road
is the only way out.
I cycle its snaking
verdant roads,
where every car threatens to push me
bushward on every glance at my phone.

His road is up ahead,
a road, not an estate.
a house, not a tower.
Every house on this neat street

has a neat lawn
and a neat car in the driveway.

There are no communal bin areas,
no shouts and screams,
no blasting radios,
no Union Jacks-St Georges
hanging in any of the windows.
This neat road is quiet.

His house.
Neat like all the others.
A dull dirty car
squats outside the garage.

The curtains are askew
in some of the windows
where boxes are piled up in the rooms.
The bins outside the house
are heaving with cardboard
and bubble wrap.

My mouth feels dry.
Every muscle telling me
to jump back on the bike
and ride back to the station.

But under it all is a dream
of my father opening the door
and welcoming me with open arms
and a wink-in-mirror smile.

THE CROYDON SOW

I hear her before the door opens,
smell her – all grunts and shit.
She can't have lived here more than six months
but already the house is heaving.
A pig sty.

I'd heard of hoarders,
seen them on the telly,
wrapping the world
around themselves
tighter and tighter,
searching for a hug
that was always denied.

She opens the door
a crack – pushes it through the muck.
Small, piggy eyes
squint out
into the odoriferous daylight.

Her eyes meet mine,
something like a smile
snakes beneath her nose
as she walks backwards into
the piling gloom
and against better judgement
I follow.

LAIR

I follow her bulk through the gloom, squeezing behind
the ever growing piles of junk: a pram atop a washing
machine in the hallway, a stack of nursing magazines
balanced on a tower of buckets, boxes for bandages, a
playpen holding bundles of adult-sized nappies.

The front door is lost to me, the shadows start to sink.
I narrowly miss her turning off through a narrow gap
between two broken flat-pack shelf units holding jars of
brown bubbling liquids. We are in what must have been
the front room. She points at a sofa covered in cat hair
and dolls.

I clear a space and sit, start to apologise, start to explain
why I'm here, that I was expecting my father, but
already she is shuffling away from me again. In a thin,
green stained dress that clings likes a second skin
against her mass.

She is back moments later with a letter, my letter, my
handwriting but the paper looks far older than it should
for something sent weeks ago. "You got the letter. You
know why I'm here?" She smiles and her canines overlap
her scaled lips. *"I know many things."*
"Does my father live here? Where is he?"
"No he doesn't live here."
I apologise for wasting her time, I get up to leave,
believing Moth found the wrong address. *"He doesn't live
here any more, dear, but this was his house. Tea?"*

I sit back down, as cat hair and dust tickle my throat. She walks away again, disappears behind a mound of cages stuffed with baby clothes. Leaving me in the dank of the room. The light is stained, it's hard to make out where the windows are — behind that pile of twitching bags? Hidden by that tower of mannequin legs?

A statue sits on a stone? Coffee table? A woman with legs splayed, scaled and clawed, wrapped by a serpent, its mouth writhing, its eyes blood-red jewels. Staring at them makes the beat of blood in my ears become a river.

She trot-slithers in, holding a tea tray pinched in meaty claws. She lays out the filthy pot and tea-stained mugs...

'You're My Cup Of Tea'
'Tea Makes Me Pee'

She smiles her needle teeth as she pours, the tea boiling from the spout. *You search for your father but you've found me, again.*

"I don't know you."

"Oh deary, you did, or you will."

The room darkens around us, the steam from the tea filling the air, the white glint of her eyes becoming brighter, the thin material of her caked dress swimming over her body.

"Who are you? What are you? Where's my dad?"
I scream at the thing shifting and slithering in
front of me as the saggy face and jowls extend
from the neck longer and longer, her dress now
scaled skin, bristling and plated, her face both
pig and lizard.
Her body in front, her body behind, above,
below, grunting and hissing.

"You searched but
it's brought you back to me,
a nightmare forgotten,
a dream not yet lived.
Another turn of the spiral,
another twist, another offshoot
of the maze. Did you kill me?
Or believe me?

Did you hear me or murder me?
Doesn't matter – you did both
and I react to all reactions
here where they meet.
Needing revenge, wanting to reward,
having to terrify and inform."

"I'm sorry, I just came for my father." I scream into the darkness, standing to run but every twist and turn is blocked by thick serpentine coils, her voice circling me.

"You came for your father
but you found me,
tooth and claw,
snout and venom.
You searched for a father
but forgot a mother,
you journeyed for masculinity
failing to see
the manhood in womanhood.
Thinking you are one thing,
disregarding what makes you whole,
has brought you to me,
saviour and monster,
pig and lizard,
reality and myth."

Her face snaps down out of the darkness, human eyes rolling above a piggish snout framing an unhinged jaw that slathers and yawns my way. I duck and tumble, scatter and run, push past a tower of books, trip over a leaning filing cabinet, scatter a column of CDs. Dim stained light pulses up ahead, I head for it, skirting a mountain of clothing and tumbling out through the front door.

The return to reality spinning my head as much as my stomach with its over-brightness. From the door behind me I see her. A fleshy smile hangs on her now all too human face. As she slowly closes the door.

Immediately it is opened again by a very ordinary-looking woman. "Can I help you?" she stutters. The hallway is bright white behind her, clear of mess. Two children clinging to her legs. I wipe my eyes and stand on shaking legs. I tell her why I'm here. "Oh, you should speak to the lawyer, he sold the house to us for your dad. Let me get you his card. Are you sure you're OK?"

I mutter a thanks, as I take a new clue in my hand, grab my bike and cycle away as fast as I can.

THE THiCK-SWEET SMELLS OF MY MOTHER'S KiTCHEN

I sit in the kitchen
as Mum cooks.
She's making one of my favourites again,
it slowly dawns on me
that she's been doing that a lot recently.

As spices and thick-sweet smells
fill the air
she tells me about the loan.
A loan she can't afford
to get me a computer I need.

"I know you love that typewriter
but really you should have a computer."

She's starting a new job
in a care home,
asks if I will meet her
on the night shifts
and walk her home.
She doesn't like
being alone in the dark.

"Of course," I say.

Remembering her other night-shift jobs
a few years back
when I would walk her back
along the night-coated roads,
and how back then, at times,
it felt like we could talk
orbits around the moon,
laugh about anything,
make up songs and giggle over the traffic.
And she could do no wrong.

I wish I could tell her of my search,
of the things I've seen,

but it feels like a betrayal,
feels like a scream – that she's not enough.
Like I'm venturing where she can't follow.

I don't know when it changed,
when the weight settled in my chest.
Was it the truth revealed?
No, it happened long before,
when the books I read
made me alien,
inked a dissatisfaction through me.
Why did I ever need more
than the thick-sweet smells
of my mother's kitchen?

AN EARLY DRAFT

Mr Addo says
I might have bitten off
more than I can chew
but thinks I can handle it.

Says he likes the pantoums
and how their repeating structure
mirrors a labyrinth's twists and turns.

He says my writing is good.
"An exemplary piece of work."

Allen comes in to ask Sir a question,
Sir starts bigging me up!
In front of Allen,
the cleverest kid in class.
Proper saying...
"Theo has done something very special here."

Allen's normally all right with me
but I can see him looking at me different,
like he can't believe that I'd be good at anything.

"Little bit more refining to do,
but it's looking really good, Theo."

I start class feeling happy,
then stupid for being so happy,
and wonder if this is what it's like
to have a father say well done.

THE FOURTH LABOUR

The laughter goes on and on.
It takes Sir ages to calm us down.

"So basically..." says Nigel,
"this Sciron man would sit by the road
and ask people to wash his feet
and when they bent down to do it
he'd push them over a cliff?"

Mr Addo nods, a smile creeping
under his glasses.

"And when they're falling,
with their cheesy hands,
thinking, 'Why did I wash
some wasteman's feet?'
they don't realise that in the water
is a monster turtle
waiting to eat them up."

Sir gives a theatrical clap.

"You've got it in one, Nigel,"
he says, laughing.

CHAPTER 11

THE MINOTAUR'S STORY - A TEEN

INTO THE LABYRINTH

I look down at my nurse,
as she gathers my few possessions
in tear-stained armfuls.
Books, mostly books.

There is excitement in the air,
I can smell it in the thick stench
of human sweat
that permeates the palace,
and a name – Daedalus.

He has finished something.
Drums are playing outside.
Crowds are gathering.

It takes twenty armed guards
to drag me from the nursery
I long outgrew.
My books are scattered,
and that's when the tears fall.

They chain me,
prod me with sticks
out of the palace
and along streets I've never seen.
I always dreamt of going outside,
of feeling the wind
and listening to the air.

All I can feel are the stones
that the disgusted crowds throw,
all I can hear are the names
that the disgusted crowds press on me.

I am led to a sunken structure,
into a room where an empty doorway pulls.

The word
L A B Y R I N T H
is carved above the opening.
A panic crawls up me
as I stare into that blackness.

Ariadne is shouting from the side-lines,
shouting to me,
shouting at the guards,
beating at Mother and Father,
telling them all to set me free.

I am thrown inside,
braying and bellowing,
begging and brawling,
apologising for existing,
saying I will do anything.

As soon as I cross the threshold
I am enveloped in a sucking darkness.

There is something not right with this labyrinth.
The entrance is gone,
my voice echoes around me,
unable to escape.

I flounder in the darkness,
lost.

CHAPTER 12

THESEUS AND SCIRON IN MEGARA

A STRANGE SOLICITATION

Theseus has been travelling for days,
ignoring the blisters
his sandals have fathered.

Sciron is a mystery to him,
the stories he has heard
are absurd.
The travellers he passed
spoke of the missing,
said, "Beware the cliffs
that overlook the sea.
Lest you go missing too."

The only clue
was a name – Sciron.
Travellers spoke of an old man,
sunburnt and twisted,
and his continuous call
to all...

"Please wash an old man's feet."

The travellers Theseus would meet
laughed in the telling.
"As if we'd wash his feet,"
they chuckled.
But Theseus suspected
this strange man
and his strange solicitation
were linked to those who were lost.

AN OLD WARRIOR

Theseus arrived at the cliffs of Megara
that overlooked the sea.
He hid behind a gnarled stump
to uncover the mystery.

Old man Sciron arrived,
a wooden bowl in his stony hand.
He sat overlooking the sea
and called across the land...

"Who will wash my feet?
Who will comfort me?
These feet have battled foes,
have won you your safety."

Theseus noted the scars
that mapped the old man's skin,
a veteran of the battlefield,
a warrior has-been.

Sciron was broken but strong
like an old temple door,
just seeking a little comfort
in his last days away from war.

But maybe he has seen
where the missing go.
Maybe this old soldier
has some clues to bestow.

Theseus meant to question
but then a woman came near.
She washed the soldier's feet,
Theseus' eyes began to blear.

Theseus watched the pair,
thinking of his mother and his home,
the journey he'd been on,
from boy to a full man grown.

Theseus watched this old warrior,
happy to see himself in him,
wondering what man he'll become
when old age finds him.

"When glory has left me
and I'm poor by the side of the road,
I will still earn some comforts,
my scars will prove an eternal ode."

Sciron suddenly shifted,
inexplicably kicked,
the woman fell from the cliff,
a sight impossible to predict.

Theseus was astounded,
shock tumbled into dread.
He couldn't comprehend the action –
what lay in that old warrior's head?

He ran to old Sciron,
who stood smiling at the sea.
"Why do that?" asked Theseus.
Sciron said, "For the Gods, not me.

I've spent my life in battle,
proving myself a man.
That life has left me nothing,
was that always the Gods' plan?

The waves hide a beast of Poseidon,
I feed victims to him in the sea.
My hope, in feeding the monster,
is that the God will hear my plea."

From the waters came a hissing,
a sea turtle of monstrous size.
It swallowed the woman whole
with mad and furious eyes.

"You're a murderer," said Theseus,
"no god will hear your prayers.
I thought you were a hero,
not a filth-foot wretch running scared."

Sciron gave an old man's sigh,
with swimming eyes that understood.
"I've spent a lifetime fighting.
I've lost sight of what's bad and good.

Perhaps Poseidon will forgive me
if I offer one last feast.
May my soul find mercy
as my body feeds the beast."

POSEIDON'S BEAST

It stares
through its mouthful
chilling me with new thought.
What does it mean to be a man?
Don't know.

CHAPTER 13

THEO AND SCIRON THE LAWYER

SCIRON - THE LAWYER

His office is full of turtles.
The man sits behind a huge desk,
looks like it's been carved from rock.
Under his desk
I can see his feet,
his bare feet,
trousers rolled up,
plunged into a tiny bubbling foot spa.

"Excuse my feet."

He chuckles.

"Doctor's orders."

His secretary paddles into the room,
a small man,
green in pallor,
offers a sea of swirling teas
with wide scaled hands,
his huge dark eyes
revealing their orbs.

The lawyer is all a-grin
as foot-spa bubbles and steam
effervesce at the back of my throat.

"What can I do
for you?"

The secretary hovers hungrily by the door
until Sciron the Lawyer dismisses him
with a wet look.

"I'm searching for my father.
You helped sell his house."

SO, LET ME GET THIS STRAIGHT

Brisk Summary

I was the solicitor for your father's house sale,
you say you're his son.
You want me to give you his address?

Yes!

You discovered that I was his solicitor
by visiting the other party in the aforementioned house
sale. A Ms. Phaia of Croydon gave you my details?

Yes!

And you believe yourself
to be my client's long-lost son.
Although you have never met my client,
nor he you?

Yes... Well, maybe when I was a baby.

So... no.

But still you want me
to hand over a client's personal details,
which I am not permitted to do.

Well I thought that perhaps...!

But, refutio! You will say that you are his son
a propos entitled to these personal details.

*Well, I just wanted to see if, maybe... I mean... like
if you could...*

Do you have evidence of the begetting?

Eerm...No!

Therefore I am not at liberty
to give you his personal details.

But...

The law is clear.
However, perhaps there is something
I could do for you....

A FALL

My stomach starts to flip
as I peer down into the uncertainty
of the words rushing up from his mouth
sentences whistling past my ears
that I don't fully understand
I'm falling, trying to grasp at meaning.

He talks about privacy laws
and guardianships
DNA Tests
and child support
birth certificates
and rights and violations
and I feel like I can't breathe
as a smile emerges from the puddle of his face
as I fall from the heights of his knowing...

I *didn't mean to...*
I didn't realise that...
I just thought I could...
I never knew that...

The secretary is back,
placing a watery green tea by my side,
his dark soggy eyes alight with mirth
as the two chuckle while I plunge.

"But perhaps there is something
I could do for you.

For a fee of course.
Write your father a letter
and I will pass it on."

An ocean of understanding
is rushing up at me...

How much will it cost?

His smile sinks
into the lowest areas of his face.

"My feet give me issue,
the bath keeps the pain away,
but nothing is as effective
as a good foot massage."

He lifts the gnarled bones of his toes,
the yellow dead skin of his soles,
the knots of his thromboid-laced ankles,
out from their bubbling bath.
Wiggles them suggestively
above the bubbling waters below.

Should Theo...

rub the lawyer's feet?
➤ **Go to page 200.**

tell the lawyer where to go?
➤ **Go to page 204.**

RUB HiS FEET

His secretary
pushes me gently from the chair,
a claw in the small of my back,
paddles me over to the desk
and presses down on my shoulder.
I am kneeling,
the bubbling foot-bath by my knees.
Lawyer Sciron's knuckle-bent feet
hovering above, dripping wet,
calloused toes stretched and expectant.

There's nothing wrong with this –
              I tell myself.
Just massaging feet, Jesus washed feet!
They're just feet and in return...
he'll send my letter to my father.

I lift my hands up.
Both Sciron and his secretary are silent
but I can feel their smiles,
like being watched by devils
as I lift a pen to sign their book.

His feet are mapped in thin blue veins,
despite being soaked,
I can see the skin is dry and flaking.
Sores linger at the corners of his toes,
varicose veins hug the bumps of his ankles.

I plunge my hands first into the bubbling bath
as if the bubbles can somehow coat them,
provide some sort of barrier...

I'm surprised at how frail his feet feel
as I start working into the arches,
pressing the balls of the big toes,
squeezing the joints whilst ignoring
the sound of his quickening breath.

When all is done,
the secretary hands me a white towel
from a cupboard of neatly folded white towels.
Sciron smiles profusely, his rock-cracked teeth
muttering promises of messages being sent.
But I'm not listening – my hands feel dry and itchy,
seem too red, like sores might be forming.
I sail out of the room, my heart squalling.

➡ **Go to page 202.**

JOURNEYING ALONE

I'm on this journey alone
no one asks if I'm ok
no advice or good ideas sown
I'm on this journey alone.

I'm on this journey alone
each step I tread is mine
my guilt seeks to be atoned
I'm on this journey alone.

I'm on this journey alone
no letters through the door
no reply for a lost-son grown
I'm on this journey alone.

I'm on this journey alone
no one to share the load
shame has become moss-grown
I'm on this journey alone.

I'm on this journey alone
as weeks trudge into months
the lawyer was my last milestone
I'll end this journey alone.

I'll end this journey alone
what kind of son am I?
With disgust a foundation stone
I must end this journey alone.

Dead end. Try another path.
➥ **Return to page 198.**

TELL HiM WHERE TO GO

I stare at the bubbles
of his foot-bath,
hear the plinking of their boil
and they connect to something deep inside,
a raging roar....

My words spoken in my way
come gushing forth,
shouted words of the estate,
forbidden words of the playground,
words spat by my grandmother
and sworn by my mother,
words of strength and power.

Words of argument and insult,
words of youth and fury,
shaming words, truthful words,
they flow from me in unabating torrents,
cascading down the walls of his shit little office,
spraying up into the face
of his feculent little secretary.

Words that pierce through the bullshit
of his imagined stature,
words that crumble
his fragile institutions.

The words come with such force and power
that as I leave his soaked office
with its reams of paper
and outdated fax machine and ugly computer
I am struck by how relaxed my throat feels,
how unscathed.
The words I spewed
were not shouted,
they were too weighty for hurling,
my words were sharp and precise,
whispered and deadly.
Feminine and masculine and my own.

SESTINA

Sir spins a new form to learn,
a *sestina*,
where the end words repeat
from stanza to stanza,
it makes my mind whirl thinking about it.

Sir laughs, says I've hit upon something,
says the form hides a spiral.
He draws a spiral through the poem,
showing the journey of an end word
as it spins through the poem,
its meaning changing, its emphasis growing,

Sir challenges me to write one
but it seems too hard,
too complex,
I like free-verse,
I like the freedom,
I like my writing to be free,
not constrained or trapped.

Sir says that's wrong,
that form doesn't trap,
that there are patterns in life,
a spiral that threads through the universe,
a spiral that connects
people, places and situations.

A spiral that connects
to the actual corkscrew orbit
of our planet around our wandering sun,
that connects the spiral arms of our galaxy
as it traces its own trajectory
through the bulk of the universe,
that connects our lives to each other
through parents,
through generations,
across time and through multiple dimensions.

"All that from a poetic form!" I say.

"Yes," says Sir as he stands, pirouettes
and tells me to roll off to my next class.

CHAPTER 14

THE MINOTAUR'S STORY – BECOMING A MAN

DARKNESS BECOMES ME

The darkness becomes me
seeps into my pores
flows through my veins.
It talks to me in the Labyrinth
drawing me to its centre.

There is a power here
that Daedalus was not aware of.
Something in the layout
of this place
the impossibility of the angles
the paradoxes of the shapes
something has opened here
down in the darkness
and is calling to me.

The Labyrinth's centre has me
and there it shows me things
worlds laid upon worlds
time laid out
like a corridor I can clop
like a valley I can scramble
I see all things here
past and present and future
combining as one.
Spiralling one atop and inside the other.

I see my bull father being swirled
into existence by Poseidon.
I see my mother's shameful longing
for him.

I see a boy on the road
fighting his way to his father.

I see another boy
in a different time
searching for his father.

All of it collides in my bovine mind
stories and lives
fathers and sons
men and gods
twisting and competing
down the darkness of the Labyrinth.

Where my twisted form
watches.

CHAPTER 15

THESEUS AND CERCYON, THE WRESTLER KING IN ELEUSIS

CHAMPION KING

It was night,
but sweat still dripped
from Theseus' sunburnt face.
Eleusis was up ahead,
a town known for its balmy nights
and scorching days.

He heard it before he saw it,
a murmuring of voices
pumping through the still air,
up and over the night-hot hills.

It took everything to climb
the last hill on his path,
the sweat waving over his body
but offering no release
in the humid buzzing air.

An amphitheatre
blinked open ahead of him,
thousands of people
lining its eyelids,
countless torch lights
adding to the unbearable heat.

A small woman runs onto the stage....

"Ladies and gentlemen,
it's time,
you've waited long enough.
Our leader,
our king,
our champion of champions...

Cercyon."

THE SOUND OF A KING

The amphitheatre falls silent.
Theseus plops down on a seat.
A woman accords him dried fruit and nuts
from a clattering clay pot.

"This is going to be good," she whispers,
her eyes drummed to the stage.

"Have you heard of our king?
He is scintillating, shatters anyone
who dares challenge him."

Theseus grips the hilt of his father's singing sword.
Could this be the king he'd heard of?
Cercyon steps up onto the hush of the stage.
A chair is intoned at its centre.

Theseus is discordant,
he's heard of a king who wrestles
his opponents to death,
but this king is drum-skin old.

Cercyon shuffles onto the chair
in his blue and purple ensemble,
waving at a cheering crowd.

A drum beats,
silence blankets the audience.

"This is it," buzzes the woman.
"He'll pluck someone and that's it,
they'll be beaten."

A question bubbles in Theseus' throat.
How could this ditty of a king
wrestle anyone to silence?
But then he records
the rows of muscle-composed guards –
clangorous around the periphery of the stage.
Understanding dawns
as Cercyon points his jangling finger
towards Theseus.

ATTACK

Theseus is pushed and pulled
to the stage by an over-excited crowd.
Stripped of sword and club,
impelled towards a stool
opposite the king.

Kindly rheumy eyes
look him up and down.

Theseus has an eye on the king,
an eye on the burly guards,
an eye on the crowd.

He rips off his shirt,
revealing the muscles
the road has given him.

The king responds
with a quizzical smile,
stands up from his chair.
Taller than he looked from
the auditorium.
He stands over Theseus,
rolls the sleeves of his robe
over arms that look deceptively strong

and attacks!

RiDDLiNG

"My light is hidden by the day
at night I help you find your way
I'm always near yet far away.

What am I?"

Cercyon stares Theseus down.
Theseus blinks,
unable to comprehend.

"Come on, lad," whispers the king.
"This is a riddling match
and my people expect a show!
Guess just one correctly and you'll win."

Fear plummets like lump-ice
into Theseus' stomach.
He was ready for battle,
muscles primed to wrestle,
not to outwit.

"Can I hear it again?" he stutters.
The crowd explode into laughter.

"That's not how it works," says the king
as a scoreboard of one-nil is paraded around.
 "The answer was of course..."
Cercyon gestures to the audience
who call en masse... "STAR!"

Theseus shrinks on his stool.

Cercyon circles the boy,
arms spread to a loving crowd,
and charges...

"My leaves are not on any tree
but many trees exist in me
and though my leaves dislike the sun
they burn bright for everyone.

What am I?"

Theseus doesn't think,
he blurts out words...

                              "Cactus."
                              "Sunflower."
Each one is met by a laughter-explosion,
each suggestion making him smaller...

                              "Mistletoe."
                              "Apollo."

Cercyon does a cheering lap
of the stage, pumping his arms,
making the crowd go ecstatic.
"Nope, it is of course..."

The crowd roar... "BOOK!"

The scoreboard does another lap.
Two-nil.
Sweat is raining into Theseus' eyes,
his head hurts from thinking.
Cercyon is all smiles.

"This last one is a special one
especially for you," he says,
aims and fires...

WHAT AM I?

"My meat is strong but never cooked
my morning crow is seen but never heard
I have a juggler's tools but never juggle
I have whiskers but never fur.

What am I?"

Theseus has thumb and forefinger
pressed to his bridge,
massaging his temples,
weapons forgotten.

He chooses not to blurt out,
chooses to sit and think,
using muscles he hasn't worked
since being tutored in Troezen.

He re-walks the riddle,
mentally sidles over to 'strong meat'
that is never cooked?
                Something that's eaten raw?
Takes a side-step to an unheard 'morning crow'?
                Could that be sunrise?
                But how does that relate to raw meat?
He skips over to 'a juggler's tools' and something clicks.
                That must be balls...?
He slides over to 'whiskers but never fur'.
                Whiskers could be a beard!
                What has balls and a beard? A goat!

But a goat's meat is cooked!
He backtracks to 'morning crow'.
A cock crows... A cock... balls... a beard!
He races back over the riddle... 'meat... never cooked'
A man's meat is never cooked!
A man has a cock and balls and a beard.
The riddle opens up in front of him,
relief showering over his brow...
IT'S A MAN!
And the crowd are with him now,
leaping from their seats,
cheering in the rows,
throwing nuts, fruit and coins
up onto the stage.

As Cercyon lifts Theseus' arm high
in victory.

A FUMBLED JOURNEY

I fumble with the cutlery,
spinning the fork in my hands,
trying to mimic
the downward stab of the other men
when all I want to do is scoop and shovel.

The king is kind,
ignores my fork as it pierces downward,
tines making a gentle hill,
that spins predictably upwards in my hands
to thrust the food mouthward.

I try to keep the tines down
but habit wants to shovel,
fist clenched over the handle
as crisped chicken,
baked fish, roasted tomatoes,
slightly salted lentils,
oils and breads are wolfed down.

"You must be hungry," smiles the king.

I nod, speaking through mouthfuls
of my journey to my father,
exaggerating my conquests,
tales of slaying and defeating.
This is a king after all,
no weakness can be shown.

"Another boy hunting manhood
on the Bandit Way," murmurs the king.

He smiles at my confusion.

"Many a boy has sought manhood
on that road,
a pilgrimage of sorts.
Many are searching for their fathers.
Many a young Athenian
travels the Saronic Gulf
for travel and experience,
sowing seeds in the smaller towns
before returning home
to marry and settle.
Years later many boys grow up
and seek their fathers
on the reverse journey,
pitting themselves against horrors
imagined and real,
trying to answer questions
that have no satisfactory answers...

"Why did my father abandon me?"
"How can I prove myself to him?"
"What can I do to be a son
worthy of a father's love?"

BATTLE-CRY

I feel the tears approaching,
an unstoppable enemy
just the other side of the hills of my eyes.
I hear the race of their battle drum,
feel the vibrations of their march
through the bridge of my nose.

I stare down at the half-eaten plate,
wondering where I can run to,
praying for somewhere to hide.

Another battalion is coming,
rushing up my chest,
my breath quickens,
there is no escape.

King Cercyon puts a hand on my back,
the way a father should.

And the tears breach all defences,
sobs raid upwards through an overwhelmed mouth.
I hear my battle-cry.

CHAPTER 16

THEO AND THE WRESTLER

THE MAP iS BURNT

The map is burnt, the trail is cold.
My father is lost to me.
I refused to take what the devil sold,
the map is burnt, the trail is cold.
My sense of loss one hundredfold,
denied the sun, who can I be?
The map is burnt, the trail is cold,
my father is lost to me.

COULD BE SAVED

Mr Addo keeps asking
about my coursework,
saying if I need help,
he can help.

Ever since the lawyer
I've gone quiet,
the excitement of the search
replaced by something angry,
something furious.

My head hurts,
on either side of my forehead
there is a sharp thudding pain.

My coursework has slipped.
Theseus kills everyone,
everyone he comes across,
like they're all bad,
like there's no nuance,
like he's perfect,
a hero killing everyone.
All to see his father.
It makes me angry,
makes me not want to write about him,
makes me fume and stomp.

But I wonder...
is that how it really went down?
Did he ever get homesick?
Did he miss his mum?
Did he ever hesitate before he attacked?
Ever wonder if the next villain
could be turned around,
could be saved?

FIRST OUT THE DOOR

I can feel the hinge of Sir's stare.
Normally we have jokes in class,
laughing like letterboxes.

But today I haven't squeaked.
When the bell goes I can feel
he's going to ask me to close the door,
to stay behind,
but I don't wanna creak about it,
anything I say would slam out of me.

I pack up my bag,
I'm the first out the door.

LUNCHTiME

Lunchtime
I have meat –
a thud of burger
with a sog of chips.

Mark asks if I'm gonna eat
the mush of cake
and can't hide his excitement
when I let him chomp it down.

"You all right?"
he asks as my knee nervously bounces
up and down.
My grandad had the same tell,
juddering the floor with his leg,
making the horses bounce on the TV
until Nan would tell him to stop.

"Yeah, course, I'm fine," I lie.
Then Addo enters the hall.

"Oh shit," I say.

> "What? Is Addo after you?
>   What you done this time?"

Mark is laughing as he stuffs
my cake mush with its pink custard
        into his mouth.

My mouth is dry,
my heart racing.
Sir will make me talk about things
and I really don't want to talk.

But he has seen me
and is coming over.

HORNS

Mark is still laughing,
pink mush all in his mouth,
the noise of the canteen getting louder:
the giggling boys,
the whispering girls,
the clatter of knives and forks
on plastic scratched plates.
Mr Addo is getting closer
and I can't stand it.
My arm jerks,
I send the bowl of pink mush
flying across the hall.
Everyone goes silent.

It clatters onto Gavin's back
and he's up
before the bowl hits the ground
all –

        What the...
           Who the...
              I'm gonna...

He's on me
in a tide of swearing,
riding the crowd's wave of...

"Fight! Fight! Fight!"

I like it.
It speaks to something in me
and I'm smiling when Gavin's fist
makes my jaw judder
and horns
erupt from my head.

WRESTLING

A crowd gathers around us,
the fighting chant filling my ears.
I'm no fighter
but I swing and hit and punch,
steam pouring from my nose,
circling my prey
with blood in my eyes.

Gavin is smiling
like he can feel the rush too
and I smile back,
feeling a power surging up
and through me,
up through the tips of the horns
that now arc either side of my head.

Mr Addo is on us,
between us,
separating us.
But I don't stop,
the horns have taken me over
in a grunting roar of searing pain.

My feet harden to hooves,
my skin erupts into a thick hair-hide.
I lash out,
one arm hooks around Sir's neck,
our legs entangle,
we powerbomb to the floor,
I want to stop
but the ring through my nose says no.
I'm moonsaulting and brainbusting.
Sir's voice is distant
like a commentator shouting at me
across the vastness of an arena
across an impossible space
across an impossible time
          getting further and further away.

All goes dark.

THEO/MINOTAUR

I'm crouched in the dark.
I stand – my horns scrape the ceiling.
I pace – my footsteps clop.

The school canteen is gone,
Gavin is gone,
Sir is gone.
Mark is gone.
I'm alone in the dark.
But the anger is still with me,
I'm bare chested.
I run a monstrous hand
over the muscles wrapping my body,
feel the thick fur
and roar a braying,
teratoid scream.

My hands spider up to my face
and meet a thick heavy muzzle.
I howl for help
but no words form
on my bovine tongue.
I thrash out,
clopping over the stone floor,
hurling uncanny fists
at the stone walls
until I fall, exhausted, a muscular heap.

My cow eyes adjust in the gloom
to the little light coming from a grate above.
My cell is round, but it's not a cell.
Six arched openings lead off all around,
each a mouth into impossible blackness,
and from one of them
I hear someone approach.

THESEUS MEET THEO

A man is formed from the shadows
with torch in hand, a trail of thread
behind him flows, I plan to shred
this lost hero from nose to toes.

I steam and crouch, brace to bulldoze
but in his eyes something unread
some prosaic thing starts to spread
his life has been the subject of my prose.

We stand together eye to eye
and recognise our twisted fate
his story mine and mine is his.

He drops his torch to verify
that strength is not borne from hate
his story mine and mine is his.

WRESTLED BY TEARS

I open my eyes.
I'm back in the canteen.
I'm out of that dark place.
I feel like I have left a part of me there,
I feel like I have brought something back with me.
An image of a boy flits across my memory,
I can't tell how long I was in that dark place.

I am surrounded
by a wall of gawking stu-idiots.
The anger blinks back into me.
I'm blinded by fury.

I am pinned but struggling.
Sir is above me, telling me:
 "Calm down."
 "You've gone too far."
 "This isn't you."

The pain in my head
is too much – I scream...

"STOP TRYING TO BE MY DAD."

The whole school stares,
watching as I'm wrestled by tears.

LiSTENiNG

The tears fall like a flood.
Sir takes me, sobbing,
through the dinner hall
and to the staffroom.
He sits me at the back by the windows
and puts the kettle on.

Miss Rutledge is all,
"Oh no, Theo, what happened?"

"Theo had a little altercation
over lunch,"

says Sir and I can't quite believe it.
Can't fathom how he isn't mad!

He brings me tea,
my head is thumping,
the horns are killing me,
with a dull thudding ache.

My body aches,
my bulging hair-covered muscles
doing nothing to ease the pain.

I lift the cup carefully
between two huge hands.
I lap the tea automatically
and before I know it
I'm telling Sir everything that's happened
and he just listens.

Listens like light listens to darkness
Listens like the sea listens to the shore
Listens like mountains listen to snow.

DEFEATING
THE MINOTAUR

Sir leaves the staffroom
and is back moments later
with the last draft of my coursework.

"I don't know who or what that was out there, Theo,
but it wasn't you, this is you."

He flicks through my coursework.

"What you have done here is brilliant.
You have reinvented the story,
made it your own."

As Sir goes through my poems,
telling me what he likes about each one,
I can feel my body shift.
The monster in me
starts to slow,
starts to stumble.

He mentions the *rondels*
and my hooves start to soften,
he talks about the *villanelles*
and my hands soften.
He tells me how he likes
the mix of form and free verse
and the hair starts to fall from my skin,
he says that my Theseus feels more real,
more like a boy in search of his father,
and my horns
shiver and shrink.

WHEN THE RAGE
HAS LIFTED

When the rage has lifted
and tears dried from your eyes
a wise word is often gifted
to those willing to apologise.

When you have raged at those who care
used their love to barb your tongue
and you feel there is nowhere
where your shame will go unsung.

That's when a friend will find you
and forgive the prickles of your voice
a friend who will teach you
that you always have a choice.

AN IDEA

I feel bad
Sir doesn't give me a detention,
doesn't send me to the head.

He just listens
and then gives me an idea,
and it's mad I didn't think of it before.

I felt like the lawyer held all the cards,
was my last hope.

But Sir made me see
that I have choices,
I've got options.

He says how when one door closes
another opens.

But that's not what gets me back on track.
As I leave the staffroom,
filled with tea and biscuits,
covered in tear-salt,

Sir says...

"Sometimes Theo, when we're lost
all we need to do is retrace our steps."

CALL OR TEXT

I want to call
but I'm too scared to call.
Maybe I should text?
Or is that weird?

Is it too soon to call?
Have I left it too long to text?

No, I should call,
but I want a favour,
but is that creepy?
I should call...
or maybe DM...

No, I'll go mad waiting for a reply,
I'll call...
or maybe I'll text.

Should Theo...

call?
➤ **Go to page 254.**

text?
➤ **Go to page 253.**

I TEXT

(message read)

Typing...

-

Typing...

-

Typing...

-

Calls to this number are barred from your phone.

A dead end.
➤ Go back to page 252.

I CALL

Her voice
lights up the line.
She flutters to my rescue.
"But I want a hot chocolate,"
she says.

DRESS TO IMPRESS

I feel stitched into the house.
It takes me forever to leave.

Trainers and jeans?
Shoes and jeans?
A shirt – too formal
A jumper – too dirty
A Pokémon T-shirt –
will she think it's babyish
or see me as being cool and ironic?

I knit my brows
trying to remember the tapestry
of her clothes.
They were so cool,
I never have any fucking money
to buy new threads,
nothing fits right.

I string together an outfit,
black jeans and a black cardigan,
Pokémon t-shirt showing through,
if I amend my mind
I can zip up the cardigan.

Last time she had headphones looped
around the lace of her neck.
Should I take my headphones?
Oh God, what should I listen to?
What music does she cotton to?
I bet she likes some well-stitched band
I've never heard of.

I take my headphones
and a spare t-shirt
in a fraying bag.

FLAWLESS

She's late
but her smile blows me apart.

"Why didn't you call earlier?
I was hoping you would."

"I didn't wanna disturb you."

"I don't give my number to anyone,
you know,
I gave it to you to use, so use it. "

She is a ruby
dark and shining.
I feel like a blind miner's grubby hand.

She is flawless:
her skin
her eyes
her smile
her style
flawless.

I can feel the new spot
picking its way out of my forehead.
Can feel the oil of my skin greasing
through the pits of my pores.

I hate hormones.

HOT CHOCOLATE

The café has closed in around us,
the windows so steamed up
it's like the outside no longer exists.

The steam from her hot chocolate
snakes up and around her,
hugging her with its sweetness.

She melts over her laptop
and marshmallows the keys,
frothing up surprises in minutes.

For a delicious moment
I forget all about the search for my father,
I'm lost in the luxury of watching her drink.

Watching her lips purse and bloom,
the way she blinks, the cocoa of her eyes,
with each savouring sip.

When she hands me the address
my head is all whipped cream and sprinkles.
I gulp my dark chocolate and scald my tongue.

"If your dad hadn't moved," she says,
"I would have got the right address first time
around.
What you gonna do?"

She reaches out a velvet hand to mine.
I take it as my tongue throbs with sugar and pain.
"I'm going to knock on his door," I say.

CHAPTER 17

THESEUS AND PROCRUSTES THE BED-STRETCHER ON THE PLAINS OF ELEUSIS

PROCRUSTES - BED-STRETCHER

On the plains of Eleusis
where you can see Athens' lights
Theseus stopped in an inn
to sleep away the night.

Tomorrow he would pound
upon the palace's gates
he would meet his long-lost father
and decide which story to relate.

But would his father welcome
or would Theseus be ignored?
Would his father recall
the buried sandals and buried sword?

The innkeeper was named Procrustes
he led Theseus to his bed
"You're looking very tired
just relax, lay down your head."

Theseus didn't argue
the road had taken its toll
and left him more confused
about his manhood-hunting goal.

He fell into a slumber
filled with every horrid dream
he dreamt of Periphetes
and his howling innocent scream.

He awoke soaked in sweat
and quickly lost all hope
his hands and feet were tied
to the bedposts with soiled rope.

Procrustes stood above him
a monstrous glint in his monstrous eye
"You're far too tall for my bed
but you're easy to modify."

He lifted up a saw
aimed it at Theseus' feet
Procrustes had done this before
his cuts would be very neat.

Theseus swore and threatened
as a rusted blade kissed his ankle skin
but nothing that Theseus said
seem to blunt Procrustes' grin.

So Theseus tried another tack
tried to temper brawn with wit
"I fit this bed perfectly
it's your eyesight that doesn't fit."

Procrustes rubbed his eyes
squinted from bedpost to headboard
"You can't trick me," he hissed
"you lanky little fraud."

"I promise it's your eyes
they're failing you by candlelight
Just wait for the sun to rise
you'll see I fit just right."

Procrustes had a ponder
then laughed with a scoff
"I'll wait until the morning
then I'll cut your feet right off."

Theseus was left alone
he braced his feet and tensed his neck
he stretched the bed's joints loose
stopping before the bed was wrecked.

His feet no longer overhung
the bed's old and creaking frame
he wondered if his trick would work
would Procrustes see through his game.

Morning came too quickly
Procrustes bounded into the room
"Now by the daylight my observations
will spell out your doom."

But confusion fell on the villain
Theseus was perfectly matched to his bed
Procrustes scrunched his eyes
scratched the thin hair on his balding head.

"I told you, it was your eyes
that fooled you in the candlelight
your eyes are making long seem short
and short seem out-of-sight!"

Procrustes, in his madness
began to pace and agonise
he brought his saw up to his face
and with its tip, popped out his eyes.

With the madman blind and scrabbling
Theseus worked loose the joints of the bed
the frame crashed around him
he unravelled free and off he fled.

Theseus knew the villain couldn't follow
but still he ran and never slowed
the insanity of violence scared him
but a lesson had been sowed.

TRYiNG TO GROW

Life puppeteered by his shadow,
an unknown man held so much sway,
I hacked and slashed trying to grow.

A hero's life is a poor show.
But lo! I see another way
from life puppeteered by shadow,

a way in which to truly glow,
to put behind me all those days
I hacked and slashed trying to grow.

To use my mind to show a foe
that use of force leads them astray,
when puppeteered by a shadow.

A glory story blow-by-blow
I will never need to relay –
a hackneyed slasher cannot grow,

a decent man cannot be sowed
when common good is left to fray.
Life puppeteered by his shadow.
I hacked and slashed trying to grow.

WITCH GREETING

At the city gates
I let my heavy club fall.
With sandals patched up
I stagger to Father's home,
and am greeted by a witch.

MEDEA

Her fingers are dyed red,
a brightness follows her,
a squinting heat.

A young boy
is wrapped around
the muscular bare leg
that shines from her robe.

She holds the boy close,
stroking his head,
her other hand fingers the pummel
of a glinting dagger.

She watches me as I ask
to see the king,
some sort of recognition
skulking behind the eyes.
            Have others come before me?

"Follow me," she flares.

I walk into a palace
bigger than anything
I saw at home.

The flap of my sandals
rings out through the stone corridors
yelling at me to run.

She leads me to a room
overlooking a verdant garden,
more plentiful than anything at home.

"Where did you say you were from?"
Her question orbits around her
as she starts to brew a tea,
mixing herbs and oils
from a dark cabinet.

"Troezen," I say, feeling ridiculous,
feeling the dirt of the road,
the weight of my sword.

"The king will be here shortly."

She hands me a steaming cup
as her boy smiles from dark eyes.
I lift it up to my mouth,
it smells odd,
too much honey
poured into something too hot.

Should Theseus...

drink the tea?
➤ **Go to page 271.**

leave the tea undrunk?
➤ **Go to page 270.**

REFUSE THE TEA

Everyone is trying to kill me,
that's the lesson the road has taught me,
I will trust the instincts the gods gave me,
I will not drink down this tea.

No doubt a poison lurks within it,
I should throw it, sling it, bin it,
I cannot just grin and bear it,
I will not drink down this tea.

The queen was not glad to see me,
I'm a threat and she fears me,
I'm certain she has it in for me,
I will not drink down this tea.

I give the cup back with a smile,
say, "I have travelled many miles
and can tell the good from the vile
and I will not drink down this tea."

Her grin is too bright and breezy,
says, "My son means the world to me."
She leans in far too casually
and with a smile she stabs me!

A dead end – retrace your steps to page 268.

DRINK THE TEA

I don't want to be rude.

So I touch the cup to my lips,
inhale its strange scent.
The queen is leering,
a smile too bright to look at.
Her son is restraining a giggle.

I smell a heady mix of floral and sweetness,
of spice and danger.
I came here to meet my father,
I will not begin proceedings
by refusing hospitality from his queen,
by letting the suspicion of the road
follow me into my father's kingdom.

I start to tip the cup,
feel the liquid sloshing forwards
when, from nowhere,
the cup is smacked from my hand.

A FATHER'S TEARS

The cup smashes on to the floor,
its foul tea fizzing at the stone,
bubbling and stinking.

My father stands beside me,
shorter than I expected,
smaller, more tired, more weary.

Without a word
he takes my blunt and rusted sword,
turns it over in his small hands,
inspects its length,
checks that it's still true
before throwing it out
into the gardens beyond.

He places a small hand
around the back of my skull,
a skull like his.
Leans in so our foreheads touch,
gazes into my eyes
with eyes that look like mine
and whispers, "Sorry."

"Would you kill my eldest son?"
He sends a questioning look to his queen.
She gathers her boy up into her arms
and radiates away into the palace.

"Being royalty is murder." He smiles
with a smile like mine.

"I should never have left you a sword,
I should have left you a book
or a pen, a map or a telescope,
anything but the bloody legacy of a sword."

I tell him of my journey,
of my desire to make him proud,
and watch shocked
as tears soften the grey of his beard.

He tells me of his legacy,
of what war and swords have brought him,
a marriage he is too scared to leave,
the people he's too weak to lead,
and the blood that they yearly bleed.

AN UNTHINKABLE TASK

A war was fought,
a war I lost
and for that defeat
an unthinkable cost.

To the victor,
the King of Crete,
I yearly send
an unthinkable treat.

The future of Athens,
its innocent youth,
are sailed to Crete
for an unthinkable truth.

Seven boys and seven girls
are led to a feast
to be sacrificed
to an unthinkable beast.

Eight foot tall,
the body of a man
but a creature's head —
an unthinkable plan.

Two monstrous horns
and steaming snout,
the head of a bull –
an unthinkable shout!

He feeds on our people,
Athens wears a death-mask,
and so I must give you
an unthinkable task!

CHAPTER 18

THEO AND THE BED-STRETCHER

A BAG OF FIDGETS

I am a bag of fidgets
standing in the doorway
of what might be my father's house.

The houses on this street are big,
this house is one of the biggest,
more of a palace than a house.

Several cars sit in the driveway,
all shiny and fresh.
I always felt nervous in other people's cars,
always slammed the door too hard,
always felt sick.
Mum can't drive,
I think of her work-weary
night-time walks.
The evenings of interrupted homework
to collect a car-less mother
scared of the dark.

I press the doorbell
before fear has me fleeing,
I hear noises inside,
voices calling for someone to get the door,
feet running down stairs,
a house alive with family.

The door is opened by a boy,
a young boy, thirteen or fourteen years old,
his hair a mass of short dreads.
Two girls stand behind,
one younger, one older.
Hair plaited and neat.

I give them my father's name,
not saying who I am,
they tell me their father is out,
but he'll be back soon.

A woman comes up behind them,
she has the phone cradled in her neck,
she smiles enthusiastically,
mouthing that I should wait inside,
silently apologising for being on the phone.

The front room is dominated by a huge TV,
the biggest TV I have ever seen.
The sofas are massive and cream
and I'm scared I'll dirty them,
terrified I've walked dirt into the house.

The boy (my brother?)
sits opposite me, grinning.
He asks my name
and I tell him and watch
as not the slightest hint of recognition
passes his bright eyes.

My sisters ask
why I want their dad.
I mumble something
about being in the area.

Notice the prettiness of their smiles,
the way they chuckle like me.

I scan the room,
my eyes fill up with the masses of photos,
weddings and parties and holidays,
grandparents, aunties and uncles.
I think of the tininess of my immediate family,
how all the cousins and uncles and aunties
emigrated years ago,
how I've never been to a wedding,
never cried at a funeral
or sat on a plane,
how small and lonely my family is.
How when a family is broken
so much can be lost.

WAITING FOR MY FATHER

"Would you like a drink?"

she mouths from the kitchen,
phone still tucked
into the cradle of her neck.

She lifts up box after box of herbal teas
with strange, potent names,
expecting me to pick one.

I think of my coursework,
I think of Theseus
in his father's palace,
I think of queens and poison.

"No, thank you," I say,

licking my lips,
feeling the parchment of my throat.

OH!

He rolls into the house,
dumps keys in bowl,
throws jacket on hook,
plants kiss on wife's cheek,
drops bags of shopping on floor.

"You have a visitor," she mouths.

I see my father's face
for the first time
and begin the process
of rubbing out
the invented mental image,
not like Sir,
not tall,
not muscular,
head not shaved,
not confident,
not certain,
not sure.

"Hello," he says,
smiling uncertainly.

        "I'm Theo."

"OK."

        "Theodore."

"OK?"

        "Theodore Andino."

"Oh!"

My mother's surname,
my surname, brings a tsunami
of understanding to my small father's face.

Something like pride
rolls across his eyes
as I tell him of the last year,
of the twists and turns,
double backs and dead ends
of my search for him in the maze.

"I would have done the same," he smiles.

And all I can think is – *but you didn't.*
You didn't search for me.

SNAPSHOT

A snapshot
of me and my father
doesn't exist.

I'd like it to be this.

He composes himself next to me
on the blank sofa
I'm afraid of dirtying,
a pile of photo albums by his feet.

He's shorter than me
but I feel tiny.
Find myself glancing sideways,
marrying his profile to mine,
between page turns.

"These are your uncles,
this one still lives in Jamaica,
these are your cousins,
this is your aunty...
this one was very successful,
this one had two degrees."

He reels off snapshot histories
of family members,
I see my eyes,
     my smile,
        my slouch,
reflected back at me
in generations of men and women
I've never met.
As a picture of family starts to emerge.

SiBLiNGS

I'm asked to stay for dinner
by a wife whose smile is too big.

The little boy shows me his room,
he has his own!
A room overspilling with toys
I used to pore over in magazines.

The younger sister wants me
to read her a story.
The older one interrogates
my music tastes.

"So, you're like a long-lost son,"
she states, eyeing me up and down.

Raised voices from downstairs
have my heart pushing
at the boundaries of my chest.

   "We knew this day might come"

comes sailing up the stairs and...

   "Thought that was the end of it"

corners through the corridors...

"What does his mother want?"

reverberates off the walls...

"But he's my son."

My siblings start showing me
the pride of their bedrooms,
the models built,
the pictures drawn,
the photos taken,
the instruments played,
the awards won,

as the overheard voices
become absorbed by the brickwork
and we laugh together,
finding a language that is all our own,
touching the words brother and sister
to the tips of our tongues.

PLANTAIN

They sit at a table to eat,
I think of the collection of trays
we have at home,
for balancing on knees
in front of our small TV.

A stool shorter than their chairs
is found for me and balanced
by the corner of the table.

Bowls of food
steam the table.
Chicken, rice 'n peas,
yam, plantain, hot sauce
and pumpkin.

"Do you eat plantain?" asks the wife,

showing teeth
that can't fit in a smile.

I've eaten plantain before,
though I pronounce it
like a word I've read
and not heard.

"Yeah, I eat plantain," I say.

"It's pronounced *plarn-tin*."

Her smile breaks the borders of her face
as she alludes to my whiteness,
to the dissolution of my black skin,
to a separation from culture
that I don't need reminding of,
that has ridden me since birth,
since a whole family was denied me.

BED-STRETCHER

It's late.
I am told I can stay the night,
that my father
will drive me to the station tomorrow.
I want to go home
but feel too shy to say what I want,
too scared to disagree
with anything that is stated,
too curious to leave.

I'm told I can sleep
in my little sister's old nursery.
The bed is toddler-sized.

"You might have to curl up a bit," says my father,

bringing in cushions
and foot stools,
trying to make the bed fit me,
trying to find space in his home for me.

I lie awake in the dark,
hearing their voices rise and fall,
hearing terse tones and arguments,
hearing talk of DNA tests
and child support,
of suspicions and fear,
when all I ever wanted
was to know my father,
was to find myself in family.

As I turn and twist,
the footstools move from the bed,
the cushions work their way to the floor,
the bed refuses to fit me.

WINDING HOME

As he drives me home,
in a car! His car!
My father regales me
with tales of family...

of distant lands that bear our name
(but it's not my name, I think),
of great-uncles who made fortunes,
of relatives that brushed fame.

He gingerly places me in the story,
tells me how he and my mother met,
how young they were,
how stupid but in love.

Tells me how he used to visit
when I was a baby,
how his mother held me once
and claimed me as grandson
(but I don't know her name, I think).
Before things went sideways.

How he wished things had been different,
how it was no one's fault,
how he's glad I searched,
how he is proud of me,
proud that I took the risk,
proud that I began this journey.
How he is proud of me.

As I stare from the car window,
thinking about the last year,
flashes of memory zip through me.
A gentle pain burns
either side of my head,
the ghost of horns.
I remember the dark place
when I went psycho with Sir
during lunch at school.
I start to remember what I saw
in that dark place.

CHAPTER 19

THESEUS AND THE LABYRINTH

SACRIFICE

The cries of the boys and girls
are never-ending.
Our journey to Crete was
carried on tears.

Seven boys and seven girls
to be offered up as sacrifices
to the Minotaur,
to pay for my father's loss in war.
I am one of the boys.

We are held in a large room,
where King Minos inspects us.
His wife hovers in the doorway,
an indescribable look on her face,
something like pleasure and shame.
She never comes near, just watches
as we're bathed and fed.

A dark doorway leads off the room,
it is the start of the Labyrinth,
a vast impossible maze,
made by the genius Daedalus.
Once in there is no way out,
and at its centre lives
the Minotaur.

Minos has heard about me,
is impressed that my father
sent his own son to Crete,
jokes how it's a clever way to
be rid of a bastard.

Little does he know what I plan.

ARiADNE

Ariadne sees through me.
When her father is done inspecting
she enters with genuine concern,
talks to the boys and girls
with long soothing tones,
with tears in her eyes
that seem real.

When she gets to me
her tone changes,
iron finds her eyes,
metal inhabits her mouth.

THE WAY OUT

Do not kill my brother
he didn't choose to live this way
he is a victim just like you
you can choose another way.

Do not enter with your sword
do not venture with your shield
there's a way that we can all win
there's a way to make him yield.

Remember that he is trapped
and is scared and alone.
Who wouldn't become a monster
with the Labyrinth as your home?

Who wouldn't attack and slay
when your only food is alive?
Who wouldn't become a killer
when you must kill to survive?

Take this ball of thread
and I will keep the other end
it will lead you both to the exit
and then this slaughter will end.

It will lead my brother to safety
bring the monster back to the light
for too long he's been hidden
to save my parents from his sight,

to free them of their shame
of the laws they chose to violate
they hid away a son
chose to dehumanise and isolate.

Do this and we will flee with you
to start our lives in distant lands
you have the means to change things
the way out is in your hands.

THESEUS ENTERS THE LABYRINTH

My father's sword
newly sharpened feels useless
as I stare into the void of the Labyrinth.
No one has ever come out.
Nothing escapes its singularity.

I will be first to enter,
entering at night before the guards wake
and push us forward.
All Ariadne's plan,
she tiptoes in, barefoot
in the black of night,
grabs hold of the thread's end
and tells me to hurry.
I need to find the centre before daybreak,
before the guards wake
and send her off to her father
and rob me of my anchor.

One step over the threshold
is all it takes.
I'm plunged into sinking darkness
as time and space merge,
all is dark, darkness envelops,
the thread floats off behind me
into impossible blackness.
I call to her but my voice
seems to hang in the air,
seems to stop and reverberate against itself
like hitting a stone wall
and then is sucked
into the darkness ahead.

A SWORD FOR A TORCH

I'm all fingers and shadow steps,
feeling my way left, then right,
up and down,
at times crawling
through things wet and dark,
at others traversing,
back tight against roughly hewn walls,
hugging back away from some
incredible depth.

Stairs of nauseating proportions
lead me up,
sickly-angled ramps
take me down.

Panic is walking its filthy fingers
up the veins of my throat.
I hold it down
but I've never known darkness like it,
eyes open or shut makes no difference.
I clamp them tight
to keep a ragged grasp on my sanity.

I kick something,
bending, I feel
the unmistakable outline
of bones and rags.

I wrap rags around a thigh bone,
strike my father's sword on the hewn stone.
It clatters, a dying rasp, several times
before sparking into life
and snapping in its own light.
The sparks ignite the rags.
I swap a broken sword for a torch.

THESEUS AND
THE MINOTAUR

I hear a noise in a room of shadows.
I extinguish my torch, hold tight the thread.
I see a hulking beast, his eyes are red,
his body steams beneath ragged clothes,

a ring insults his grunting nose.
A grate above alights his bed –
a mass of bone and hay stained red.
I slow my breathing, try to compose

a gesture that is not a threat.
I forward step as his bellow roars,
avert my eyes, crouch to the sand.

With a bone I scratch, in alphabet,
his sister's name upon the floor,
look on up and offer my hand.

THESEUS, THEO AND THE MINOTAUR IN THE DARK PLACE

Being here feels
like being in the eye of a storm.
The beast looks up at me,
something human in his eyes.

"Your sister sent me,"

I say,

"I'm here to get you out."

I show him the thread,
he reaches out a thick hand
and suddenly we're both risking it all,
both trying not to be the hero or the monster,
each searching to be a different kind of man.

He shifts, he changes,
through him I start to see another:
    I see a boy
    maybe my age
    he is looking at me
    through the Minotaur
    and for a moment they are one

the boy and him
horned and scared
eyes like mine.

I reach forward, needing to connect,
feeling the thread vibrating in my hands.
I stretch,
he reaches and we are connected.
Everything is still at the centre of the Labyrinth.
Time has stopped in this dark place
as we stand where dimensions kiss.

We tell each other of the strengths of our mothers,
of the power hidden in words and riddles.
We share the vulnerability we feel in love,
and the pain hidden in force and brutality.
We talk of our fathers,
men flawed and scared,
broken and trying.
We tell each other it's OK
to be scared, it feels great to cry
and that when we search for anything
we'll always find ourselves.

CHAPTER 20

THEO

A NEW CORE

My father empties me
at the station,
eyes worried and tired
but proud.

He says he'll see me soon,
tells me not to come to the house though,
says its hard on his wife.

Shifting uneasy every time I mention
my mother.

"Your mother knows I'm married?"

I almost laugh
as I watch the fear
at the centre of his eyes,
scared of losing what he has,
unable to fight for what he's lost.

"Don't worry, Dad,"

I say.

"This was all my idea
and there is nothing I want
but to know you better."

I see the little boy in him calm.
Feel my back straighten,
feel something solid shift
within me,
feel the ghost of horns,
feel the monstrous muscle of a heart
that has grown.
A core I didn't know was there.

I pat him on the back
as I leave the car,
I tell him it's going to be OK,
    I tell him our journey is just beginning,
        I tell him he has nothing to fear.

A WAY OUT OF THE DARKNESS

As my coursework emerges from
the new computer and printer
my mother enters my bedroom
to watch the spectacle.

"Is this for school?"

she says, lifting the pages
with fearful wonder.

I tell her it's my coursework.

"But these are poems,"

she says, mouthing the words as she reads.
I scoop up the manuscript,
ordering its pages.

"I always liked poetry at school,"

she says.

"Before I left, that is."

I offer to read my poems to her
and am taken aback when she nods.

I read her my take on Theseus
and though I don't mention my journey,
don't want to upset her with
talk of my father,
I see the understanding
roll over her face.
And as I read tears start to fall,
mine and hers.

I keep reading,
she keeps listening,
we laugh through the tears,
grab tissues and continue,
smiling and blowing our noses,
reading and listening,
knowing and understanding,
feeling our way out of the darkness,
finding a way to be mother and son.

THESEUS IN GREEK MYTHOLOGY

Like many of the Greek Myths, the Labours of Theseus are not set in stone.

Sometimes Theseus is referred to as the son of the King of Athens, at other times he is the son of the god Poseidon. His journey around the Saronic Gulf has been described as both a task to rid the road of bandits and a journey past the six entrances to the underworld. And each character he meets has different interpretations…. Was Phaia the name of the Crommyonian Sow or of the woman who owned the pig-beast?

These varying interpretations come about because the stories have been reimagined by many writers with different intentions for over two thousand years, writers who themselves were most likely referring to long-forgotten works. The ancient Greek historian, Plutarch, often refers to multiple interpretations when describing Theseus' journey, from both written text and hearsay.

But yet, despite the thread of origin being web-thin at times, the thread remains, because there is something in these stories that connects, that speaks to our inner selves, that spoke to me. It was this thin thread that I let guide me – the story of a boy searching for his father.

So I have taken some liberties with the story (or rather held true to the tradition of multiple narratives).

My Theseus does not merely kill each bandit he comes
across as per the "original" interpretations, for I find
it hard to believe that such interactions would go so
smoothly or be so black and white. Instead he goes
on a journey and changes and is changed by it. The
bandits are not just targets to be mowed down, they are
flawed humans with their own histories and their own
labyrinths to weave.

And then of course there is the Minotaur.... I have a soft
spot for this poor beast who is so often painted as a
bellowing brute, whilst the monstrous acts of his parents
are so often confined to the bottom drawer. So I took
great pleasure in giving him a voice and a backstory,
recasting Ariadne as a sister who actually cared for her
half-brother, and allowing the Minotaur to escape from
the maze.

Joseph Coelho

Praise for
The Girl Who Became a Tree

'Accessible and powerful, an imaginative and exciting narrative which is a thrill to read aloud' – *BookTrust*

'Coelho's story in poems interweaves the ancient myth of Apollo and Daphne with a nuanced study of grief and isolation, to absolutely stunning effect' – *Waterstones*

'Heart-breaking, powerful, totally involving and engrossing, with evocative illustrations from one of our most innovative illustrators' – *Tricia Adams, LoveReading4Kids*

'A highly readable, imaginative tale with a positive message. Succinct, thought-provoking and original' – *The Independent 10 Best Kids' Poetry Books*

'Plays with form and setting in a way that invites young readers in, asserting the Daphne myth's perpetual resonance' – *Imogen Russell Williams, Times Literary Supplement*

'Combines intense imaginative power with brilliant poetic technique in a multi-layered story of loss, deception, recognition and ultimate reconciliation' – *Fiona Noble, The Bookseller*

'This is wordsmithery extraordinaire' – *Teresa Cremlin, Open University*